FATE'S BANE

FATE'S BANE

C. L. CLARK

Tor Publishing Group
New York

This is a work of fiction. All of the characters, organizations, and events portrayed in this novella are either products of the author's imagination or are used fictitiously.

FATE'S BANE

Copyright © 2025 by C. L. Clark

All rights reserved.

A Tordotcom Book
Published by Tom Doherty Associates / Tor Publishing Group
120 Broadway
New York, NY 10271

www.torpublishinggroup.com

Tor® is a registered trademark of Macmillan Publishing Group, LLC.

EU Representative: Macmillan Publishers Ireland Ltd, 1st Floor, The Liffey Trust Centre, 117–126 Sheriff Street Upper, Dublin 1, D01 YC43

The Library of Congress Cataloging-in-Publication Data is available upon request.

ISBN 978-1-250-29314-5 (hardcover)
ISBN 978-1-250-29315-2 (ebook)

The publisher of this book does not authorize the use or reproduction of any part of this book in any manner for the purpose of training artificial intelligence technologies or systems. The publisher of this book expressly reserves this book from the Text and Data Mining exception in accordance with Article 4(3) of the European Union Digital Single Market Directive 2019/790.

Our books may be purchased in bulk for specialty retail/wholesale, literacy, corporate/premium, educational, and subscription box use. Please contact MacmillanSpecialMarkets@macmillan.com.

First Edition: 2025

Printed in the United States of America

10 9 8 7 6 5 4 3 2 1

To S

CLAN ARADOC

The Collar

The first time I saw Hadhnri Clan Aradoc, Second-Born Pedhri Clan Aradoc, it was dark and I did not know her. I was lost, in a stranger's roundhouse, in an enemy clan's territory, far from home—far from my father, my brother, my mother-brothers and father-sisters all, who had sung me the songs of warm hearth and battle glory since I was a babe.

How could I know who she would become to me when I barely knew myself?

I was led along with the other slaves that clan Aradoc had taken, stumbling through the wetlands in my boots, which I was allowed to keep, but no coat, which had been stripped from me. I didn't complain. I was too frightened to complain, though later I told myself I had been too brave.

The Aradoc warriors led us to the clan roundhouse down a path lit by their torches. Our steps creaked over wooden planks drawn across the sucking mud and peat. The blood flies buzzed and bit at my ears, and across the night, the frogs croaked and splashed into the water, the crickets clapped their legs together, and all around me was the drone of the fens in lententide, underlaid by the trill of pipes. The songs by which I knew my clan were gone, replaced by the music of the Aradoc fens.

A shivering bundle of men, women, children, we huddled in the roundhouse. The sulfur scarce covered the blood-and-sweat odor of our unwashed bodies. Others, unlike me, held themselves high-chinned and sharp-eyed, despite their exhaustion. They knew themselves, name and clan. But I did not know myself and because I did not know myself, I had no pride to hold me up.

I knew myself only as chafed and starving, filth-crusted and fear-stinking.

Arranged on their benches and furs, Clan Aradoc leered at us. The long-legged hounds at their feet stopped their bone-worrying to snarl low in their throats, teeth gleaming, hackles ruffled.

In my shivering, I didn't hear what pronouncement Pedhri Clan Aradoc, the new chief among chieftains, made over our fates. It wasn't until the slaves around me drew back that I attended his words. He ordered me alone to stand before him, and I obeyed. He took my chin in his callus-grip hand and looked into my eyes, my teeth, my ears. He checked my scalp, snarling my hair. His eyes were a glowing hazel, his brown beard sparking red in the light of his clan's hearth.

Something passed between him and one of his men, because I was then taken away to be scrubbed with a scouring rock, my head shorn like a lamb, and my clothes replaced with comfortable, dry wool. I was too numb to notice its quality, and how it differed from the clean roughspun the other slaves were given.

In the roundhouse again, they fed us thick broth, rich with the marrow of salted mutton. I gulped it down and spent the rest of the night in the slave corner with my knees curled up tight to my chin, protecting my gurgling belly.

For most of the night, no one else spoke to me—not until Hadhnri did. She came to me as a shadow, backlit by the flicker and flash of the hearth. She came to me and, with wide, round eyes, traced me from the top of my shorn skull to my wool-socked feet.

"You." She pointed at me and crooked a finger, so I unfurled myself and stood, looking up at her from below my lashes.

She was my age, perhaps a year younger or a year older. We were of a height, though she was already wider than me at the shoulders. I could not tell yet how cruel the edge of her smile would be. I couldn't make out the sweet brown of her skin, dusted with freckles, nor the yellow-green-brown of her eyes. Nor did she yet have the crooked cast of a broken nose, or the scar that would split her lip, a gift I would give her. What she did have, though, was a straight-backed pride and a solemn demeanor.

Her eyes stopped this time at my neck. She reached

out with her fingers, and I flinched when she brushed the leather collar locked at my throat. Unlike the collars of the other slaves, it was studded with copper. It splashed fire across the dark roundhouse whenever I moved. Gone, all chances of sneaking.

I flinched, though her touch was gentle as a feather-kiss.

"You are Agnir Clan Fein, First-Born Garadin Clan Fein."

From anyone else, it should have been a question, but from Hadhnri it was a statement. She named me and I came back to myself, enough to straighten my shoulders, for I was my father's child. She took it as an answer.

"You are not a slave," she said, "and will not sleep with the slaves. You are my father's ward, and he will keep you as such. Come with me."

I followed Hadhnri into my new life.

The Tale
Goes like This

Once, we were all one clan, led by mighty warriors.

Once, we were all one clan, living as peacefully as we could within the Fens.

Once, we were all one clan, plagued by the witch of the Fens.

The witch—who may not have been a witch but a demon—who may not have been a demon but a god—who may not have been any of these things at all—was the guardian of the Fens and claimed our ancestors as trespassers.

Many mighty warriors attempted to kill this creature to free us from the black eye of its attention, which drew ill-luck: children, drowned in a handspan of tepid water; legs of men and legs of beasts, sucked into the muck to break; disease, passed from family to family to family.

They called it trickster, they called it the luck-hound, they called it fates-bane.

Warrior after warrior bent their shoulders to the task, but always something went wrong. The hilt of a sturdy blade came apart right before the killing blow. A twig cracked or a waterbird splashed, giving away the creeping warrior's position. The string of a bow snapped and took out the archer's eye.

No one succeeded until one man, Bannos the Clever, Bannos the Bold, strong and cunning, turned his ill-luck against the fates-bane. For his victory, Bannos became the clan's leader and led it into prosperity, following the cycle of the land.

In this prosperity, he had many children, and in the way of siblings born to power, they did not agree who should succeed their great father. When Bannos died, the clan split and split and split along the lines of his children and their most loyal. The seat of Bannos's power—the heart of the Fens, where the earth is richest, the peat plentiful—has passed between the splintered clans several times since then, ever at the point of the sword.

That is the tale as we heard it from our fathers and our father-sisters in Clan Fein.

That is the tale as we heard it from our mothers and our mother-brothers in Clan Aradoc.

That is the tale, say the tale-tellers of Clan Elyin and the song-singers of Clan Hanarin.

That is the tale, say the lore-makers of Clan Pall.

That is the tale of the Fens.

The Spring

We became fast friends, Hadhnri and I. We took our chores together, hauling bricks of peat and replacing the rushes on the floor of the roundhouse; we practiced the different trades of the clan, rotating from leatherwork and fishing to smithing and weaving; we trained daily with seax and axe and sometimes even the sword, trailing along behind Gunni First-Born Pedhri Clan Aradoc.

Gunni had a few years and a handspan's height over us, with handsome features that the clan gossiped about; some blushed and giggled behind their hands. Like Hadhnri, he was generous with me, teaching me weapon-work as they learned it in Clan Aradoc. Their way was not so different from Clan Fein, but I was eager to learn.

Though they were both kind to me, the tension between the siblings was blood-thick, and never more so than in the little patch of grass that served as our training grounds. I said that Gunni was kind; he was kindest when it was the three of us alone. With his age-mates around, or Pedhri

Clan Aradoc watching, he would sacrifice us—especially Hadhnri—on the altar of their approval. It was after one such time, perhaps a year after my capture, that Hadhnri and I fled the Aradoc roundhouse.

"Wait!" he called after us as we ran, our wooden seaxes pumping back and forth at our sides. "Come back, or you'll get the hide!"

We didn't go back. We ran rabbit-fleet and deer-sure over the wet pockets of the earth. Already, with Hadhnri as my guide, I knew the land as if it were my own.

My hair had only grown back to a short cap of dense curls, but Hadhnri's flew behind her, a cloud of red. Though we'd fled in indignation and frustration, the more we ran, the less helpless we felt. The crease in Hadhnri's forehead, the jut of her lower lip—they both gave way to grin, her eyes squinting as we rushed against the wind.

Even a river must slow, though, and so did we, legs jangling from a gallop to a canter to a walk. With wind-chapped cheeks and cold-split lips, we stared at each other, chests heaving with this newfound might.

We had said *no*.

Behind us, far, far, far away, I saw a smudge of what might have been the roundhouse and the smoke of the fire rising like a streak of cloud. Before us stretched a carr, the sedge meadow that we'd run through, turning into a forest of skinny birch, reaching naked-branched to the sky. Fog shrouded the ground up to our knees.

The Baneswood.

Hadhnri's thoughtful pout returned.

"Should we go back?" I asked. Already, I would have followed her anywhere, even there.

Hadhnri's frown deepened, and she rubbed her backside—without realizing it, I think—where Gunni had smacked her needlessly hard that morning, humiliating her in front of the clan after she'd let him get around her guard. He'd paddled her bottom like a child.

"No."

Together, we entered the luck-hound's wood.

As many trunks that stood tall, there were those that had fallen sideways—some dead and some growing twisted and determined. We clambered over and under the ancient yews and, once, rode one like a horse. We whiled away the hours, roaming deeper into the woods, pretending to battle each other across the rough terrain.

Deeper and deeper we went until we could no longer see the hill from which we'd come. Moss muffled our footsteps. We crouched like hunters through hanging willow fronds, holding our wooden seaxes up like spears.

"Agnir. I'm hungry," Hadhnri confessed.

"Shh." I pressed a finger to my lips. I stopped and hunkered lower at the burble of water.

"What is it?" Hadhnri bent close beside me, our shoulders knocking. Her breath tickled my ear.

"A creek, I think? Or a spring."

"There are no fresh springs on Aradoc land."

But we crept closer and lo, sheltered beneath the trailing fronds of a willow—as a lover is sheltered by the curtain of their love's hair—a spring. Just stepping near to it gave me a chill; that is how cold it was. I could see down to the gray-brown stone beneath; that is how clear it was. The water rushed from its source and down some path of root and tangle. I considered following it to see where this spring-that-was-not-Aradoc's would take me.

Hadhnri knelt beside the spring and fanned her fingers into it. She closed her eyes and sighed. It looked wonderful. I followed her, instead.

The water was as cold as the air around us promised. My eyes widened with shock before I closed them in quiet reverence. It wasn't the frigid cold of a slip into the fen's marshy waters, unpleasant, unfiltered. This was the cold of waking after the first frost, when every breath is new-scoured by the ice in the air.

Later, when many details about this day had faded, I always remembered one thing, sharp as the leather knife at my thumb: I drank of the spring first.

I cupped the liquid to my mouth and sipped. It tasted as pure as it looked. No sulfur stench, no mud grit. Crisp, like an apple, and sweet.

"It tastes like strawberries." Hadhnri grinned into her own cupped hand.

"No." I laughed, scooping another drink. "Apples."

Hadhnri splashed me with wet fingers. "Strawberries!"

We splashed and drank and laughed, shouting each new taste we discovered in that delicious moment.

Belly-full, we settled, lying on our sides in the loamy soil, our fingers trailing into the water. I had missed my family, when I had gotten over the shock of becoming Clan Aradoc's ward. I'd been angry that my father surrendered me, that he had not fought harder for me. But as I sat with Hadhnri Clan Aradoc beside that spring, all I wanted was to be near her. For her to like me, no matter that I was First-Born Clan Fein.

"Do you think the clans will ever unite again?" Hadhnri's voice was soft and somber, all her exuberance gone. If she had been the warrior before, slashing at the undergrowth, she was the solemn clan leader now. She gazed into the distance, perhaps all the way to the future, while she wove strips of grass unthinkingly.

"Maybe. My father won't fight your father as long as he has me. We're at peace."

Hadhnri's hands stilled on the grass braid. "We're not united."

The water ran cold against my fingers. I thought of the pools in parts of the fens where the surface of the water was still as stone until a fish broke the surface or a frog leapt out. How the creatures must squirm and struggle beneath the surface no matter how quiet it appeared.

"You're right. Maybe there's no peace either." I sat up

and hugged my knees to my chest. An emptiness stole through me. "What will happen to me if there is no peace, and my—and Clan Fein attacks Clan Aradoc?"

Hadhnri didn't speak the obvious truth: that my life would be forfeit. My father had not said so when I left, and Pedhri Clan Aradoc had never admitted it as he sat me at his own table, dressed me in his own wool, or trained me with his own weapons.

The line between Hadhnri's eyebrows returned, and I had the strangest urge to press it out with my thumb. So I did.

She jerked, startled as a goose. My smile was self-conscious, but hers was not. Her mouth stretched, wide as a wound.

"Agnir." Hadhnri's eyes burned wolf-bright, now brown, now yellow-green. She took my wet hand in hers. "Name me a hero of the Fens."

I was happy to turn the subject away from our melancholy, but I was confused. "What?"

As she looked from me to the spring water, however, I understood. I bent over and cupped more water in my hand, and stood, trying not to spill a drop.

Hadhnri knelt before me. She kissed the blade of her wooden seax before plunging it into the lush earth at my feet. She placed her hand on the pommel and bowed her head. I let the cupped water trickle over her, and it ran from her hair, down her brow and her nose.

This was how a person became an adult and took their proper place in the clan. I placed my hand over hers on the seax.

"I am Hadhnri Clan Aradoc. By my name and my clan, I pledge myself to the keeping of the Fens and to their people. To their fish and their fowl. To their beasts and their burdens."

She spoke not like a child of thirteen but like a full member of the clan. How many times must she have heard this speech in the tales of the heroes Aradoc? The tales of Bannos the Bold?

"By your name and your clan, you honor us, Hadhnri Clan Aradoc." I smeared my other hand wet across her forehead. If it were fenswater, as it would be when she was named true, a streak of mud would have marked her, but her brow was clean.

Then Hadhnri looked up at me, earnest-eyed and solemn-mouthed. Beads of water caught on the pale brown of her crinkled eyebrows. "By my name and my clan, I pledge myself to you, Agnir Clan Fein."

I cocked my head. "That's not how it goes."

"It is," she insisted. "Will you accept my oath and let me rise?"

"Rise, then, hero of Clan Aradoc." I mimicked the gravity of a roundhouse pronouncement by Pedhri Clan Aradoc—and to a lesser extent, Garadin Clan Fein, whose voice I already struggled to recall.

I offered both my hands to raise her to her feet. Standing, she was almost unbearably close to me. Her eyes held mine. She clasped my hands tightly. I kissed first her right cheek, then her left, as was correct to honor a hero of the clan—

And then she kissed me on the mouth, her lips spring-wet as she pressed them, closed, against mine.

The baying of hounds and men broke the joy-spell between us, and another spell, also—for we both grew aware of the chill and the dark, and the gurgle of our hunger returned. The wood around us was cast in shadow, the gnarled trees ominous instead of adventure, fear speeding our steps instead of exploration.

We followed the alarmed voices until we saw the glow of torches waving through the birches. As we neared the edge of the wood, the dogs howled, but they didn't enter the trees after us. They waited, looking from the clan members in the search party to us and whining.

They jumped on us with muddy paws when we broke from the trees, claws scratching. The world rushed back as if a gauzy film were pulled from my eyes. Though it was dark, color returned.

Pedhri Clan Aradoc loomed, sword in hand.

The Punishment

He yelled at us both, a great belly-roaring, but most of his ire was for me. I led his child astray. I almost cost him his dearest treasure. The fens are dangerous in the darkness, even to those who know their paths, and the Baneswood— all knew the luck of the fates-bane.

"We were safe, Aradoc-Father," I said quietly, bowing my head. "We stayed to the solid paths."

"It was clear, Father. All the way to the spring."

I inhaled sharply. In her dutiful honesty, Hadhnri had confessed something I knew should have stayed our heart-secret, more dangerous than the kiss we'd shared.

"There is no spring in the Baneswood," Pedhri growled. He turned to me with his full body, and the weight of his regard sat heavily.

"I thought so, too, Father, but there was—"

"Go, Hadhnri." Pedhri did not turn his gaze from me.

I bowed my head lower. From the corner of my eye, I saw Hadhnri's eyes widen in understanding, then the resolute pout of her lips.

Don't, I willed toward her, but it did not reach.

"Father, there *was* a spring, I swear it on the bones of—"

"Hadhnri!" Pedhri jerked his head at one of his men, and the man looped a thick arm around her. He lifted her feet off the ground and carried her into the roundhouse.

Pedhri guided me away from the light of the fire and into the darkness. The flap of the roundhouse fell, cutting me off from the warmth, and the stirring hearthsounds, and Hadhnri's grunting struggle. The cold stole into me as it hadn't before, and I immediately began to shiver. Aradoc-Father gripped my shoulder, his large thumb finding the hollow of nerves there and pressing.

"Where did you take my child?"

"To the spring, Aradoc-Father." I gritted my teeth through the spasming pain in my shoulder. I was not a warrior, but I had puffed up my pride as much as Gunni had in our weapons practice. I tried to bear this punishment in hopes that Pedhri would see I could be trusted.

He slapped me across the face, knuckle-backs crashing like stones against my cheekbone. No inflated pride could stop my head spinning or wash the bright metal of blood from my mouth.

"You will tell me the truth, Agnir Ward-Aradoc."

I dug the toes of my boots into the earth. They were crusted in fresh mud. If only that were proof—but the fens were full of mud. If only we had brought some of the water with us, honey-sweet, to share, but it would've trickled through our hands, quick as our joy.

I weighed silence against a lie; the lie measured safer. "Nowhere, Aradoc-Father. We wandered the fens."

"Until after dark? When you should have returned to the roundhouse?"

"We lost track of the sun, Aradoc-Father. We were careless. I am sorry."

"Why did you go, Agnir? What were you doing?"

"No reason, Aradoc-Father. Only to—to play. We were tired of the lessons, and Gunni, he—he slapped Hadhnri on the arse with his practice sword. We were angry."

"What did you do with my child, when you led her away?"

I looked up then, eyes wide. "I didn't hurt her, Aradoc-Father."

This time, his knuckles knocked me to my knees. My fingers splurged the wet earth. Pride gone, I sniveled and reached my muddy hand up to my pain-hot cheek.

"Did you lay a finger upon Hadhnri Clan Aradoc?"

I was young, but I was not a fool. I closed my eyes tight and thought of the gentle press her of lips on mine and the bird-wing flutter in my belly. My cheeks ached then like they did now, burning from blush and aching with grin.

When I opened my eyes again, Pedhri Clan Aradoc glared down at me like I was filth. He'd never looked at me like that before, not even the day I arrived as a slave.

The sweet truth of that moment in the spring would only hurt more if I spoke it here.

"No, Aradoc-Father." I hung my head and pushed myself to one knee before him.

He grunted. After a moment, he raised me by one arm and then tilted my chin up to the light of the moon. I blinked to hold in my fresh tears.

"You will not touch my child ever, First-Born Garadin Fein. It is not your place. She is not for you. Understand me." His voice was hard as stone, but it was not unkind. The warmth of a hearth-brick could make you feel steady and safe, and it could burn. It could crack your skull.

"Yes, Aradoc-Father."

Pedhri scrubbed his hand affectionately over my head and patted my shoulder before returning to the roundhouse.

I followed him, hiding my face, already swollen as a plum. Though Clan Aradoc stared as we returned, no one gainsaid his treatment of me. I went straight to my furs and buried myself in them, turning my back to the rest of the roundhouse so that they would not see me cry. Though my stomach growled and then cramped, I refused to rise.

They whispered in reed-wind voices of the spring that Hadhnri and I couldn't possibly have found and the fell provenance of it. They sang of Bannos the Clever and the fates-bane, and with every telling of the tale, I felt their eyes upon me.

With my own eyes shut, a shadow fell over me, darkening the red of my eyelids. I curled into myself. A hand upon my shoulder and I knew who it was. Pedhri's warning throbbed in my head. I recoiled from Hadhnri's touch.

"Agnir?" she whispered. "I brought you dinner."

I wanted to turn to her. I wanted to read the concern in her voice writ across her face. I wanted her to put her hand on my shoulder again.

I hunched deeper into my furs and remained that way until her absence grew cold at my back.

The Attraction

Years passed. Garadin Clan Fein—or "Garadin Fein!" as Clan Aradoc liked to curse his name—did not attack Clan Aradoc or encroach upon the allotment of its fens. I grew taller, though not much taller. I settled on the path of the craftsman; no warrior, I, though I was competent enough to split Hadhnri's lip in the training yard. She taught me how to disarm Gunni, and Gunni humored me, laughing, when I tried. Near-grown, he began to court and be courted by young women and men—within Clan Aradoc and without. They brought him love-locks tucked within gifts of leather or wool to signal their interest. Never a suit from Clan Fein, though.

One year, a wave of bog fever took infant and elder and almost took Pedhri Clan Aradoc's pregnant wife. She survived; the babe did not. Pedhri glowered in the roundhouse then, and more cursed Garadin Fein in my hearing, the continued existence of my clan a failure that brought ill-luck upon him.

It ceased to bother me, for I was distracted.

I had begun to notice Hadhnri in a new way. She'd

developed the same muscles I'd once admired so in Gunni; only, I had wanted to emulate Gunni, to see those muscles swell beneath my own skin, hard as stones beneath flexing flesh. And I had! I knew well the strength in my back and my legs. But with Hadhnri, I felt different.

I was finally able to name what I couldn't as a child: I *wanted* Hadhnri, not only because of the deep, ever-certain timbre of her voice or her quick laughter and quicker kindness. It wasn't because she was skilled with axe and leather needle or deft in the dancing ring. I wanted her in the way of other adults, in the way of nights beneath furs. I wanted to run my thumbs along the swell of her arms and press my lips there. My tongue ... I rarely allowed myself that thought unless I was alone; I had learned, as well, how to subtly ease the ache I felt after a long day at Hadhnri's side.

Despite the glances I had caught from Hadhnri, as furtive as my own, I kept my feelings from her. I had not forgotten Pedhri Clan Aradoc's knuckle-crack warning against my cheek. No doubt it would be worse now; I was no longer a child with innocence as excuse.

I sought other occupations for my hands, but Hadhnri had ever been braver than me. She could afford to be.

She found me one day as I carved the face of a dog into a block of wood. The snout wasn't right—it was too fox-sharp, but to shave it down farther would dull definition I'd already cut.

"That looks like Ha'Blue."

I startled at her voice and turned to where Hadhnri

knelt beside me. In the clear sunlight of early lententide, her hair took on the red-brown of her father's, and her hazel eyes turned like harvestide leaves from brown to ocher to mossy green and back again. Her smile showed a crooked eyetooth beneath her scarred lip.

Her smile fell and she took my hand, holding it to her. She rubbed away the upwelling blood. "I'm sorry."

"Don't be." I hadn't noticed. My face was aflame, but I was too sunstruck to turn away, to take my hand back. "Do you really think it does?"

"Yes." She pointed with one finger at the carving, but she didn't release my hand. "The muzzle wrinkles just like hers."

"Oh." I looked back down at our hands and started to pull away. She held me fast.

"Come to the workshop with me?" At my hesitation, she added: "I'm working on something new. I could use your help."

I hesitated, still. She held me, still. Then she rose, bringing me up with her, and led me to the workshop, my mouth dry as hay.

The clan sparked with life that lenten noon. The smoke from the roundhouse chimneys smelt of rich peat. I took a deep breath and let it settle over me. Rinach, one of the elders who minded the children, shouted from a chair in front of the roundhouse while the children ignored her warnings. They blurred past our knees, and Hadhnri's giggle echoed theirs as we dodged their tiny ferocities.

Inside the workshop it was dark as a secret and just as quiet. I expected her to come to me then, my cheeks already burning. Instead, she riffled through the shelves and returned with a cut of leather and a cloth.

"Will you wet this for me?" Hadhnri held the cloth out to me as she straddled the bench.

I did. "What will it be?"

Hadhnri frowned in concentration. "A hilt grip. I took the measurements from Father's sword, but I wanted— It's for Gunni. I'll make a sheath as well."

I joined her on the bench and ran my fingers over the dry leather, taking the measure of flesh with flesh.

"For his aging day?" I asked. Gunni would be an adult soon, a full member of the clan, free to wed, to leave the clan if he wished, though that wasn't likely. He wanted to be chief of chieftains, like Aradoc-Father. Everyone knew it. A sword meant that Aradoc-Father supported that ambition.

Hadhnri's aging day would come soon after, and so, I supposed, would mine. The world would not open up to me, though. The Ene would not carry me away, its waters silver as a belly-up fish beneath the sun. Though my fingertips brushed the leather of Gunni's one-day hilt, it was the collar on my neck I felt. My throat scraped against it. It was possible, yes, that on my aging day, Pedhri Clan Aradoc would offer me a place within the clan. If he deemed me worthy. I doubted he could forget where I came from. I was not sure if I could either. For Hadhnri's sake, though? Perhaps.

"Yes." Hadhnri's eyes dropped to my collar, also, or maybe to my lips.

I sat and traced the shapes that came to my mind, where I would cut for the leather, the proportions for suppleness without slack. I closed my eyes and saw the design that would suit my foster brother. Gunni thought himself a wolf, but he was too kind for that, his smile too easy. I thought of Ha'Blue and her flopping ears, chasing waterfowl or curled by the fire. I thought of the shapes that would flow around her, balancing the movement about the hilt. I took the wet cloth and wiped the leather until it was damp but not soaked. I picked up the dullest awl and held it over the leather.

I turned to Hadhnri. "Do you want me to—?"

Her lips were parted as she watched me, and heart-flush burned my cheeks anew. "Yes. I trust you."

"If you don't like it, we can start over."

"I will like it."

Shyly, I traced the design in my mind's eye onto the wet leather, light as I could. I paused to assess my handiwork: in the thin strip, a hound head with a lolling tongue and ready ears. It was small; it had to be, to fit the flat handle. On the other side, the birds and the rabbits.

"Can you tool something that tight?" I asked Hadhnri. She was the true leatherworker. I only had the eye, not the hands. "And the lacing, here?"

She smiled at me, then brushed her fingers over the

shallow grooves. I shivered as if she'd run her fingers over my skin.

"If you can see it," she said, "I can make it."

I began to trace the rest, my belly warm and my chest full, but Hadhnri spoke again.

"Feinur gave me a lock of hair." With her elbow on the table, she faced me, sitting astride the bench as she would a horse.

I froze, my tool hovering over the leather. Feinur was the weaver's apprentice, tall and rangy, with an easy smile and a flop of thick, dark curls that he held back with a leather thong when he worked. I looked to her hands, half expecting to see the snipped curls.

Hadhnri's fist clenched around nothing.

"Will you give him one back?" The warmth in my belly curdled until I felt queasy.

"Should I?"

She held me with her eyes, asking a question I knew only one answer to.

"We can't." I swallowed, my throat thick as mud. "Aradoc-Father. He said that if I touch you—"

"On my aging day, I can go where I please. With whom I please." Hadhnri paused, biting her lip. Then, her voice rose, hopefully: "Or sooner? After Gunni's aging day."

My hand went to my neck. To the leather there, solid and warm. My second layer of skin. "No one in all the clans will remove this. They'll know me."

"Clan Fein, then. We will go to your people."

"It would break the peace." I sighed, dropping my chin as low as the collar allowed. "We cannot."

Hadhnri—brave Hadhnri! stubborn Hadhnri!—did not accept defeat as easily. She raised my chin and turned my head. She stroked up my jaw. Her fingertips were cold, and I remembered instantly the spring we should never have discovered, with its sweet, frigid water. A shock passed between us and she jerked away. But she came back. This time, she pulled me to her and pressed her lips against mine. Not swift innocence, but bold and lingering.

My breath fled and I slammed my eyes shut—why? Out of fear? Out of instinct? So that I could pretend it wasn't happening, so Aradoc-Father could not say it was my fault? Or so that I could feel more present in the heat of mouth and mouth?

Yes and yes and yes and yes. Nothing existed for me in that second but the warm breath from her nose on my face, and yet nothing waited in my future but dread that Aradoc-Father would know. That dread made a snake-coil around the glow in my belly, threatening to snuff it out.

Boots tramped up the steps leading to the workshop, and we sprang apart as Gunni ducked under the flap.

He blinked in the dimness, his thick eyebrows a low scowl. "Hadhnri? Is that you, here in the dark? Agnir?"

"Yes, it's us. We're working on something for Father, and he'd hide you if he found you knew of it."

Hadhnri—clever Hadhnri!—had disguised our hurried separation into an attempt to cover the leather on the table. It was Gunni's gift, after all. It was meant to be a surprise. My face, however, was scalding, a burning-sun wonder in the dark. I spread my hands over the damp leather belatedly.

Gunni stepped closer, and I stood, hunching over the table. I laughed, short and bright as lightning.

"Go away!" I played along. "Or we'll tell him you were nosing."

Gunni grinned back, eager. He knew what to expect with his aging day on the horizon and was torn between the desire to know and the delight of anticipation. Hadhnri and I bunched closer together to hide the leatherworking. Her forearm warmed against mine, and I melted butter-soft into her. I forced myself not to look. To watch the childish glee on Gunni's face. The plump of his cheeks had not hollowed, might not ever hollow—Aradoc-Father's cheeks were round beneath his beard, and Hadhnri, too, had a softness in her face that I wanted to brush with my fingertips.

"I'll leave you be, little shadow-wights," he said, backing away with his hands raised, while he craned his neck for a peek through the gaps between our arms. (There were no gaps between our arms.) "Father says you're not to be scheming, Hadhnri, and that he knows you both skipped weapon-work with Lughir yesterday. He says not to do it again."

Gunni finished with a grim note of warning, the heavy timbre of his deepening voice surprising them all.

Hadhnri shooed him. "I'm no sheep, Gunni, you'll not hound me. Now get out."

When we were alone again, I sat with my hands in my lap. Hers rested on the table while she idly flicked the edge of the leather I'd been drawing on. Our heavy breaths and heartbeats were the only sound in my ears. Then Hadhnri sucked her bottom lip into her mouth and reached for my hand. I flinched away before I could command my body not to.

I winced at the pain in her face. I grabbed her hand before it could retreat, but I held it low, beneath the table, as I glanced over my shoulder.

"He'll tell Aradoc-Father we were here." I pushed my curls back from my face with one hand, then clasped it back around hers. "We—we have to work on Gunni's gift. So we have something to show him. Elsewise..." Elsewise, he would know. He already suspected, or else why would he care so much for where Hadhnri spent her time?

Hadhnri set her mouth, her heavy brows in a scowl that matched Gunni's. Slowly, though, she realized I was right. Her grip on my hands slackened and she scooted closer to me while she pulled the damp leather close.

"Finish, then, and let us see."

The Making

And so we lit two rush lights and I finished tracing the outline of my vision while Hadhnri grumbled.

"He can't even lift a warrior's sword," she muttered, more cranky than truthful, for we both knew how strong a warrior he would be. "He will bring shame to Clan Aradoc. Better he keep it sheathed than look a fool."

I raised an eyebrow at her in amusement as she watched over my shoulder. She flushed, abashed.

"Fine. But I curse him still." Hadhnri laughed. "He should be shamed for spying."

Idle curses, the curses any sister would swear upon a meddling brother who had paddled her backside with a sword in their youths, or who told tales to guard their father's favor for himself. Only idle.

I laughed too. "You mean for interrupting." I looked at Hadhnri through my eyelashes.

Hadhnri traced a caress across the back of my shoulders. My eyes closed involuntarily as I shivered down to my center. She was pleased. Then she took the leather from me, and with nimble hands, used her sharp awl to trace the careful curves and lines I'd drawn with my blunt one, pounding gently with the stone mallet.

It felt strange to work with her, as if the passing of leather between us wove something deeper than the knots we graved. My skin stippled, the hair on my arms rising as if before a lightning strike. It was cold, cold as it had been at the spring in the Baneswood, but our hands were steady.

The air smelt sweet.

Time raced away from us. When we at last lifted our heads, I could tell it was dark by the changing light against the workshop's walls and the sound of voices as clan members returned from working farther afield, greeting their families and their friends. Hadhnri and I looked at each other, breathless again but giddy this time, a new weight between us. As if we *had* been together, something precious kindled between us. With both of our hands on the leather, I could *feel* her.

This time, a heavier tread stomped into the workshop, and my heart sank as Pedhri Clan Aradoc entered. He examined the table, the tools and the leather, the nearness of Hadhnri's body to mine. His brow creased and his mouth pursed, his scowl the larger, fiercer version of his children's.

"Father, look." Hadhnri stood, raising the strip of leather gingerly in both hands. It was too long, but

Hadhnri would cut it to fit the hilt when the sword was ready. The design would fit perfectly.

Aradoc-Father approached until he stood behind us, and while his expression toward me was suspicious, for his daughter, there was only warmth. He reached between us and took the leather, then held it up to his face, squinting. He turned it this way and that in the smoky rush light.

"This is what you made? For Gunni's aging day?"

"Yes, Father." Hadhnri clapped her hand to one eye and bowed in respect. "Agnir drew the design and we tooled it together."

I stayed silent, eyes lowered.

"Is this true, Ward-Aradoc?"

"Yes, Aradoc-Father." I bowed with my own hand pressed to my eye.

Pedhri Clan Aradoc set the leather gently upon the table and patted my back and Hadhnri's.

"This is fine work, both of you. Fine work. Can you do more like this?"

"Of course," Hadhnri said, chin high and haughty.

Aradoc-Father waited for me, his eyes sharp.

"Yes, Aradoc-Father."

"Good. Now come. It is time for supper. You've made me wait." He squeezed our necks and steered us, as if we were kittens.

By the time we had eaten and gone to bed, the feeling

that had overcome us while we worked together, the feeling I had first felt with her in that spring, had faded. If I could sense Hadhnri from across the roundhouse, it was only in the usual way I had always been able to find her, my lodestone.

The Strangers

Pedhri Clan Aradoc gave Hadhnri and me special requests: leather armor for this clan chief, a sheath for that one, tooled boots for this warrior, and a belt for that one. I was honored by the trust he put in me, though his eye was ever sharp upon us; Hadhnri and I were rarely left alone during the space of a working. Within months, it became known that Clan Aradoc's leatherwork was of surpassing quality, and with that interest came more trade. Clan Aradoc grew rich, richer than before as the head of the clans of Bannos.

Rich enough to draw the interest of a woman who called herself queen in the lands-beyond-the-Fens.

One day, some months after our first Making, strangers came on tall horses, wearing thin cloaks of bright cloth and buckles that shone gold as hay grass, picking their way clumsily through the fens, cursing in a tongue I didn't understand as they sank into patches of the wetlands.

They didn't belong. Gossip spread wind-swift through

the lowlands of these strangers from this Queen-Beyond-the-Fens. When we feasted them, I bore a jug of beer along with Pedhri Clan Aradoc's other children and poured for the guests while they spoke our tongue on stilt-legs to Aradoc-Father. It was hard to understand their meaning, especially keeping two paces behind the table beside Hadhnri and Gunni. They spoke of land and drainage and peat, but I could not weave together the full tapestry.

The representatives of the Queen-Beyond-the-Fens left with a leather purse that Hadhnri and I had made, tooled with a flock of herons walking through the marshy wetlands on reed-stalk legs.

Hadhnri and I made many things in those months, but we weren't always overcome by that . . . *feeling*, as we had been the first time, when we worked on Gunni's hilt. The feeling that we were more than ourselves, more even than the pair of us. I noticed the pattern first. We had made several items for the joy of the making, for the joy of giving gifts to members of the clan, but occasionally, the gifts were for those we liked less. In jest, we would utter a curse against them, and we felt a pleasure come over us. Like my secret, solitary fumbling in the dark. It made my cheeks flush hot to feel like that beside her. At first, I didn't know if she felt it, too, but the third time it happened, she let out a flustered laugh and refused to meet my eye until I confessed.

We never did it when others were working in the

workshop with us, honing or carving or mending or weaving, and there was often someone there. Chaperones, though no one acknowledged it, to keep an eye on the untrustworthy ward as I grew older and more capable of treachery. I wished to cross only one line, and Pedhri Clan Aradoc knew it well.

Though I could see how Hadhnri struggled with our desires, I was too afraid. I let her brush my hands with her knuckles. I held tight and inhaled deep the scent of her when she hugged me—we were friends, were we not? We had been friends longer almost than I had lived with my own Clan Fein. So what, if friends embraced? So what, if, in the brief moments we had alone in the workshop, with the feeling of our Making upon us, she kissed me again, feather-light upon the corner of my lips, before a chaperone could appear?

So what?

Hadhnri received many love-locks that lententide, but she did not return them, nor give any herself. Soon, I would not be the only one who noticed.

The Gift

First Sunstead came. The end of the year brought the aging celebration and the troth-lock announcements and any clan honors Pedhri Clan Aradoc chose to bestow.

The sun set on the year's shortest day to the sound of children shrilling and dogs yapping and the fire crack-popping as it burned. Soon, it would be a bonfire large enough to scour the sky and help us through the longest night of all. Over smaller fires, sheep roasted on spits and tubers boiled in cauldrons.

Inside the roundhouse, the noise only grew more condensed as we gathered. We tapped the cider barrels and the single precious cask of wine from the Queen-Beyond-the-Fens, which rumors said she had bought from the Land-Beyond-the-Sea. We grew boisterous with drink.

Pedhri Clan Aradoc called for silence, though, and the world stilled.

"Clan Aradoc," he said, stepping before the chieftain's chair, where tomorrow he would hear the plights of clan members and receive visitors from other clans or beyond.

We all raised our mugs and howled for him. This was

the joy of the day. The wildness of year's end. My blood sang with the noise, and when Hadhnri grinned at me from her sprawl-legged spot on the bench at my side, the song grew louder.

Pedhri Clan Aradoc spoke: "A true member of the clan is a shoulder for their fellow. They help us pull the weight of our burdens and raise us in our glories." He spread one arm to gesture at the youths standing off to the side of the roundhouse. Gunni and his age-mates waited gawk-eyed, trying their hardest to look strong enough for the burdens Pedhri Clan Aradoc spoke of.

"Today, another band of Aradoc children crosses into the clan fully, children no more. Who will welcome them?"

We howled again as the parents and guardians of the youths gathered opposite them, all of them bearing gifts in their arms.

One by one—except for the twins, Nocrin and Hagnor, who approached together, moving in step, as inseparable as Hadhnri and me—the youths came before the chieftain's chair, where their guardians gave them their welcome gifts. Then, the youths knelt before Pedhri Clan Aradoc and their guardians, made their oaths, and received their cuts. Last of them was Gunni.

Gunni knelt on both knees before his father, as the others had done, but there was a special quiet as he made the oaths.

"By my name and my clan, I swear to protect this clan.

With my wits and my body, I will strengthen it. In the darkness and the light, I will guide it, linked arm in arm with those who rose before me and those who shall come after."

With his keen knife, Aradoc-Father cut the crossing pairs of parallel lines beneath Gunni's left eye. Gunni accepted the pain silently. Then Aradoc-Father anointed him with water from the fens, and it dripped down Gunni's forehead, mingling with the blood down his cheek.

"Rise, then, Gunni Clan Aradoc, First-Born Pedhri Clan Aradoc, and join your clan." Aradoc-Father helped Gunni to his feet and handed him the sword in its tooled scabbard.

Gunni took the sword with reverence and admired the art of the scabbard, but he lingered longest over the hilt. Pride swelled in me. Though we had tooled the scabbard, too, it was not a Making; nothing had overcome us that day. Hadhnri and I shared a secret smile.

But Aradoc-Father was not done. "Next, we will celebrate the heroes of Clan Aradoc. Come, Hadhnri Second-Born. Come, Agnir Ward-Aradoc." He beckoned us, proud dignity.

The clan whooped as they turned to us, but we were both bewildered. It was not our aging year, and we had performed no heroic feats. While we untangled ourselves from the crowded bench and walked toward the chieftain's chair amid the staring, Aradoc-Father turned to collect two gifts from the basket behind him.

I had never expected to be brought before Pedhri Clan Aradoc's seat, especially not in honor. My eyes grew wet.

When we stood before him, he bowed his head at each of us before speaking to the clan.

"Hadhnri's and Agnir's talent has made us even more prosperous in the last ha'year. With their help, we have snared the attention of the Queen-Beyond-the-Fens, and all other clans know us as first among them. Their work is like the best of Clan Aradoc—we are strong, and we are beautiful." His solemn mien split, broken by a wolf-tongue grin and a wink, and the rest of the clan laughed. Then he sobered.

He raised one of the items in his hand. A seax with a silver hilt in a smooth leather sheath. "Strength," he said as he handed it to Hadhnri.

I looked to his hands eagerly, hoping for a blade of my own.

Instead, he held up a bright woven belt. "Beauty." He draped the belt over my outstretched hands.

Then, with a fierce hug, he crushed us both against his thick chest and thicker belly. I was grateful; it gave me time to hide the disappointment that surely showed on my face.

I mastered myself by the time he released us and offered him, and then the clan, a tremulous smile that could be blamed on my gratitude and not the falcon-swoop of my stomach.

The gifts and honors continued, but the words and

the cheering all blurred in my ears. When it was finished and time for us to eat and drink and dance the new year into being, I no longer had the heart for it.

I stepped out of the great roundhouse and stood before the bonfire. It had grown while we sat the ceremony inside. The sky above was black as pitch as the fire devoured the light of every star. It was the brightness of a new year. A new future. And the shadows that danced around that brightest of hopes? That was where I told myself I belonged. So I settled in the darkness on the far side of the roundhouse, away from the celebrants and the new adults of the clan and the newly troth-locked. I wrapped my new belt around my fist and drew my loneliness over me like a blanket.

I was not so drawn into myself that I didn't recognize the deer-step of Hadhnri's boots as she came to find me. No matter what, I could not hide from her. I did not want to, not truly, but I was embarrassed as she sat beside me. I drew my knees to my chest and laid my cheek upon my thighs.

She crossed her legs and held her new knife in her lap. Not carelessly, but not as if it were precious. Not like I would have held it. She held it as if it were already hers, had been for years. Hadhnri followed my eyes and then looked to my new belt, which I clutched in my hands.

"Your gift does not please you?"

"It is not a blade. Not like yours or Gunni's. It's not a gift for a child of Pedhri Clan Aradoc."

Hadhnri's brow knit, and I saw the words stop behind her mouth as she weighed them. *But you are not a child of Pedhri Clan Aradoc. You are just his ward. Trueborn child of his enemy.*

Hadhnri stroked the belt, tracing its intricate weave. "He cares for you, Agnir. He chose this belt because he knows how skilled you are, and because you of all people would appreciate its beauty. He must have gotten this at great cost from the Queen-Beyond-the-Fens."

I glared sullenly into my lap. In the shadows, I could no longer see the brightness of the belt's colors, but they had been so vividly dyed. Purple deep as plums and blue bluer than a summer morning. The cream threads were clean and pure as milk. Hadhnri was right. It was likely an expensive gift. But it was not a blade, as Pedhri had given his trueborn children. I jutted out my jaw.

Hadhnri nudged me playfully with her shoulder. "Besides, you and I both know that you do not want to fight."

The words stung me where I was already wounded. "You think I am not brave."

Hadhnri frowned. "That's not what I think."

"You know why he will not give me a weapon. What fool arms an enemy's whelp to kill?" I grumbled. "I've given him no reason to doubt me."

I wondered, then, if that was wrong. Should I have planned Pedhri Clan Aradoc's doom, as a child of Clan Fein? What would Garadin Clan Fein, my own true father, say if he saw his lost child so close to his blood enemy's second-born?

No matter my pain in this moment, I could not see myself hurting Pedhri Clan Aradoc. He had raised me beside his own children, fed me at his table. He had seen my worth. I fingered the braided belt in my hands. Pulled it tight and felt the supple fibers creak. To turn on him would be to turn on Hadhnri, who loved her father as he adored her. But was that enough for me to wish myself marked as he had marked Gunni, to scar me Clan Aradoc for good?

Hadhnri was quiet beside me, and all was the sound of celebration in the roundhouse. I heard frustration in her breath the way a dog's huff warns of his whine, or his growl, or his bite. I did not know which would come from her.

Without warning, she unsheathed her new seax and pressed the shining blade against her cheek. I startled, afraid she had heard the traitorous beat of my heart—then I heard the whisper through her hair, a sickle cut against high grass.

She held the lock out to me in one shaking hand. I had never seen her tremble so. Not my Hadhnri, brave Hadhnri.

I stared at the offering, my mouth dry and my stomach knotted but my heart oh so full—I had not realized until then how badly I had craved this moment while denying it, how Aradoc-Father's warning had dragged me like a leash attached to the collar around my throat.

"Will you take it?" Hadhnri asked, her voice— Fate, how it shook.

I took it. Of course I took it. I clenched the love-lock so tightly in my hand the luck-hound itself could not pry it from my grip. But I could not stop myself from saying, "We cannot. Your father forbade—"

"I don't care. I am my own. Chieftain of my own heart. Master of my own path. Not my father, and not you, sweet Agnir. I swore an oath to you once. Do you remember?"

I would never forget. "We were children."

Hadhnri clasped her hand over my clenched-tight fist. "I meant it then. I mean it now. By my name and my clan, I pledge myself to you, Agnir Clan Fein." She stared at our hands, gathering her courage for something else.

In a rush, before I could lose my nerve, I slipped my empty hand behind her head and pulled her face to mine.

How different this was from our first kiss in the spring, or that second kiss in the workshop before our first Making. Something within me snapped free at the first press of her tongue against my lips. I surged into her, trying to pull her closer, clumsy in my eagerness. I stopped once to think—*Does she like this? Am I doing it right?*— but her small sigh satisfied my fears.

Hadhnri pushed me back onto the cold ground, and I stared up at her. Behind her, the map of the sky stretched across the land, and we were all and only. She lowered herself upon me; she tasted of mead and smelt of smoke and salt and leather. Her hand tangled in my hair was an unexpected pleasure that cinched my belly tight. This was a new spell tying us together. Not a joy-spell, but something deeper. Something starved and greedy with it.

What have I done?

I had crossed a line over which I could never return. How could I refuse her, now that I had tasted her? Her mouth was as irresistible as the water of the spring. If only given the chance, I would drink her up until my belly was swollen and I was nauseous with it, and still I would thirst.

I would never be able to deny her again.

"Hadhnri," I whispered, holding her hips against mine, her love-lock clutched in my hand. "Hadhnri, what shall we do?"

She never answered me. The scuffle of boots and the boisterous jests of Gunni and his age-mates approached from the other side of the roundhouse. We rolled apart.

"My sisters!" he called, wearing a grin of smoke and swagger as he strutted with his hand upon his new sword pommel. "I have not thanked you for this handsome gift. It's well worthy of the King-Beyond-the-Fens."

His friends snickered at the long-running joke among the youth of Clan Aradoc. None of us had seen the Queen-Beyond-the-Fens, but we knew the riches her people brought us. Fine furs, gold and silver that we turned into torcs and armbands, jewels the color of berries but cold as ice, cut to refract the light as a raindrop did. Surely, we thought, she must be as beautiful? And Gunni had taken it closest to heart, his dreams shifting from chieftain to king. He was Gunni, First-Born Pedhri Clan Aradoc—his father was already married and could not take the beautiful Queen-Beyond-the-Fens to wed, but Gunni—how eligible he was!

Hadhnri and I sat apart, clutching seax and belt respectively. Gunni's eyes narrowed, his thin lips pursing beneath the pup-fur of his mustache, and I knew then for certain that Pedhri Clan Aradoc *had* bade him keep Hadhnri and me apart. And yet, I felt warm: He'd called me sister. He, at least, saw no difference between me and him, between me and Hadhnri. He opened his mouth.

"You're welcome, brother," I said, recovering before Hadhnri and couching our crime in a tease. "But you will need more than a handsome sword to be worthy of the Queen-Beyond-the-Fens."

Hadhnri stood and I followed the sway of her broad back hungrily. "And do not be too proud of your blade. She will think you are compensating for something." She slapped the sword scabbard where it rested astride Gunni's hip as she passed him. "Come along, Agnir. Let's see what food the King-Beyond-the-Fens has left us."

The Herald

The strangers from beyond-the-Fens returned as soon as the weather warmed enough to make easier travel. There were more this time, and they came on foul-tempered horses that were ill-suited to the wetlands. A young boy offered to lead them gently through the solid paths, to best avoid the luck-hound's sink-spots, and the lead rider kicked out from his stirrup, catching the boy in the ear. The child yelped and ran wailing to his father.

Tension stifled the roundhouse that night. I poured the mead with Hadhnri, but Gunni was no longer a child, and so he sat at table with Aradoc-Father and the strangers. The lead rider sat between them. His purple-and-cream robes were threaded with gold, as fine a thing as the belt I wore. Gold rings glittered on his fingers, and a gold chain dangling from his neck held one of those cold, bloody, beautiful stones. It drew my eye to distraction; I almost overflowed his mead for staring at it, and he cursed at me in his tongue.

Hadhnri put a secret hand against my back when I retreated. Though we had exchanged love-locks that

Sunstead past, we had been—tried to be—circumspect. She whispered, "Are you all right?"

I was shaking. I nodded, though, and we continued our duty.

The robed leader came with warriors, bearded men with eyes that roved and lips that sneered as they took in all of Clan Aradoc. I misliked their disdain and wondered that Pedhri Clan Aradoc accepted it beneath his own roof. He wasn't oblivious, but he laughed too loudly at the robed leader's comments and beckoned too often for food to fill the man's plate. I let Hadhnri fill his cup instead.

Gunni jested with the soldier sitting on his other side, a man with a thick, dark beard and eyes the blue of a robin's egg. Gunni had been trying to learn the language of those-beyond-the-Fens, and I could tell the warrior's jests were at Gunni's expense; Gunni's pale brown cheeks were flushed red. I was relieved for his sake when the warrior twisted his hand to call me over with the mead.

I poured, nodded my head to him once, and made to step away.

The warrior grabbed me by my belt, that beautiful belt made by some craftsman from beyond-the-Fens, and he jerked me back to him, saying something in his own tongue. His compatriots laughed, and that told me enough. I pulled back, and he yanked me again, laughing as I began to panic.

I didn't think. I was a ward of Pedhri Clan Aradoc, and he had taught me to fight. I slammed the jug down on his hand, then threw the mead into his face.

He leapt to his feet, roaring and grabbing at me, but Gunni stepped between us, one hand against the man's chest, the other reaching toward the sword at his hip.

"These are my sisters," Gunni growled, abandoning his attempts to speak the other man's tongue. "You'll not touch them without their permission."

Whether the warrior understood or not, I didn't know. He lowered his hand to his own blade and looked to his purple-robed leader. The warrior pointed to his neck, and I realized he was referring to my collar. Suddenly, it felt too tight around my neck, and my breath grew rapid. The leader scowled at Pedhri Clan Aradoc.

"Is this how guests are treated in your halls, Aradoc? Is there no comfort to be had from your slaves for men long upon the road?" He spoke our tongue with an odd accent, replacing some sounds with others. I misliked that, too, and the implication that I had done anything wrong. My face burned with a mixture of humiliation and fury.

"She is not a slave, Herald. She is my ward. Should your men need comfort, they're welcome to ask any member of the clan they wish."

The herald—I did not know what it meant, this title—spoke to his man, and the man pointed at me, leering and smug.

I turned to Aradoc-Father, whose eyebrow rose in a question. Fear clutched my shoulders, hunching me like a rabbit beneath the fox's eye. He wanted to impress these men. He wanted their connection to the Queen-Beyond-the-Fens. I was only his ward, the child of his enemy. My desires, my dignity, were not worth the ruin of this alliance.

Pedhri Clan Aradoc stood. His presence dominated the herald, who still sat, and the warrior, who wiped his face and glared between me and our respective leaders. "I said he may ask, not that he may take."

The herald's frown deepened, but he cut his hand at the warrior. He turned back to his food, picked up a slice of the roasted lamb, dripping warm, and put it in his mouth with fastidious fingers. Without looking at Aradoc-Father, he spoke around the food: "I will see that my queen hears how you have treated the servants of the god."

Aradoc-Father bowed his head courteously. "Take to her my apologies. You and your men will be compensated for your journey in other ways. You have seen the leatherwork we do, yes?"

The herald mumbled toward his plate, and Aradoc-Father turned to me—and Hadhnri, who I only now noticed had come up behind me—and nodded toward the door of the roundhouse. It was best for us to leave.

Outside, I breathed afresh, now the rabbit released from the snare. I crouched against the roundhouse wall, fear-shivering. Hadhnri wrapped herself around me, cooing so soft and so tender that she coaxed out the tears I'd been holding back. When the crying stopped, she wiped my face with her sleeve.

"I can't believe Father wants us to make them gifts."

"They can rut with the pigs if they want *comfort* so badly," I muttered into my knees.

Hadhnri tilted my chin back up. "I would make something special for the man who touched you." Her eyes gleamed in the starlight with unshed frustration. "Come with me?"

I understood. I took her hand, and she helped me up. We went to the workshop.

The next morning, we gave the herald and his party several gifts, including a handsome leather gorget traced with a wolf-knot, with the wolf at the center opening its jaws toward the wearer's throat. I personally handed that to the man who had grabbed my belt, and he leered at me when I did. I was not wearing the belt today. I would never wear it again.

They took the gifts ungraciously and passed the next few days without incident, though the warriors did eye the slaves with cruelty. It made me even angrier to know that some of them were Clan Fein, but I could do nothing more than what I had.

What I did bore fruit the day before the herald and

his men were due to return to their Queen-Beyond-the-Fens.

I was in the roundhouse with others of the clan, tracing a design that I thought would go well on a pair of boots. Aradoc-Father was speaking with the herald on the dais. The herald—his title, I now knew, meant he was some speaker for the god-beyond-the-Fens—wore bright red over his cream robes today. He looked like a crested bloodbird, and his pinched face and close-set eyes only heightened the comparison. Normally, I would have preferred to be in the workshop, but as much as the herald's presence made my skin crawl, I felt safer knowing Aradoc-Father was nearby.

A great commotion rose outside; everyone in the roundhouse startled, glancing curiously at the door. It sounded like a row. Normally, I would have shrugged it off; brawls were common in the training yard, and usually only in fun. Those that weren't were brought to Pedhri Clan Aradoc for a weighing. With the foreign warriors here and their untrained manners, I worried. Hadhnri was out there with them, and Gunni too. The shouting grew louder, frantic.

Pedhri Clan Aradoc stood just as Hadhnri ran into the roundhouse.

"Father," she said, running up to him. "There's been an accident. One of the herald's men." She glanced toward the herald but finished looking into her father's eyes. "He—was injured."

The herald puffed himself with alarm. "Injured how? By whom? Bring him at once and see to his wounds!"

This time, it was me Hadhnri glanced at first. Then she thrust back her shoulders and raised her chin. "Father, the herald's man is dead."

Pedhri Clan Aradoc stilled. It was more than ill-luck for a guest to die on your land. "You're certain?"

Hadhnri nodded.

Aradoc-Father sprinted to the training grounds, the herald flapping behind him. A few others followed, either to help or to nose like buzzards at the carcass for their gossip.

Hadhnri came to me where I sat on a bench alone. Her face was pale as ash, her freckles stark against her skin.

"What happened?" I asked.

"The one who grabbed you. He was sparring with Gunni and of course he was being a dog's whole arse—it was the gorget, Agnir." Hadhnri stared at the ground in front of her, eyes glassy.

"What do you mean?" But already I felt the answer creep up, the way you know a cloud has covered the sun without looking to the sky.

"It—choked him. First, he just gagged a little, and Gunni was able to slap him on the arse, but then he didn't stop and he fell to his knees and his face turned purple. Gunni and the others tried to help him, but the more they tried to unclasp it, the tighter it got, and his eyes, the way they—" Hadhnri covered her own eyes with her palms.

"We did that." My voice was faint with horror.

When Hadhnri opened her eyes, though, when she looked at me, the glassiness was gone. A glint of satisfaction mingled with the fear. "We did. Our Making did this."

I held my hands out in front of me, then flattened them against my thighs, as if they were weapons I could sheathe.

"Then we won't do it again."

"What?" Hadhnri pulled me around by the shoulder. "It kept you safe!" She leaned closer and murmured fervently, "Think of what else we could do!"

If it was ill-luck for a guest to die, it was worse luck for it to be a murder.

But what was luck, and who did it belong to?

"He wasn't supposed to die."

I thought of the spring in the fates-bane's wood. Our muttered curses in the workshop.

"He deserved it." Here was Hadhnri the warrior, the clan chief's daughter passing judgment. Her voice dispassionate, her face unmoved.

"Hadhnri, what if this—this thing comes from the fates-bane? We should leave it alone."

"What if it does? What if it is a gift? What if—" Hadhnri swallowed, attempting to convince herself. "What if the fates-bane is on our side?"

I scoffed. "Do you remember Fanig's little brother? Just a babe, and smothered in the night by a twist of the blankets? Tell me that wasn't the luck-hound. Or," I continued over Hadhnri's protests, "when Torvin's father went hunting in the Baneswood and never came out?"

"Tempting fate is what he was doing. You can't be mad if it calls back to you."

"And the babe?" I knotted her tunic in my fist to rein her. To keep from losing her. "Us? Are *we* tempting fate? Do we want *that* on our side?"

Hadhnri scowled. She had no retort for that. She was halfway to covering her eye to avert the fates-bane's gaze when she realized and lowered her hand in a fist.

"It saved you," she muttered. "Like we wanted."

"What if next time it's someone else? Someone in the clan? We can't control fate any more than we control the floods."

It hurt me more than I could say to cut myself off from the sweetness of our connection, especially since I would never get a chance to be closer to Hadhnri than that. But I thought of Gunni's hilt, of the countless things we'd made, the small jokes and petty vengeances we'd taken with our Makings. This was different. This was too far.

"I won't do it again, Hadhnri."

She looked at me as if I had slapped her, her wounded expression a gut slit that threatened to spill my insides.

I glanced around to make sure Aradoc-Father hadn't returned and that the others in the roundhouse were occupied by their speculations, then I took Hadhnri's hand. "Please. This power frightens me."

After a moment, Hadhnri sighed and covered my hand with hers. She brought my hand furtively to her lips.

"No more. I promise."

The Wedding

A year passed, and most of another. The Queen-Beyond-the-Fens sent more emissaries, and whatever dispute arose because of the dead warrior was smoothed over. Hadhnri's and my aging day would come at the next Sunstead, but before that came second Ha'night. As the leaves of the Baneswood changed color, it was time for those who wished to marry to pledge their troth in the sight of the clan.

It would have been little more than another celebration to me, if not for Gunni counting among them. Not to the Queen-Beyond-the-Fens, as he'd sworn, but to Efrig, a woman as tall as he but more beautiful by far. He had dodged the luck-hound, we made certain to tell him at every opportunity. Hadhnri even threatened to steal her from him if he could not please her, and they had pup-tussled in the dirt, yipping and tickling until Hadhnri begged for mercy, tears of laughter in her eyes.

Now, Hadhnri and I sat on benches on opposite sides of the room while we watched three couples take their oaths in front of the chieftain's chair. There had been drumming, but it had stopped, the better to hear the words the couples spoke. Nocrin stared at his new husband with tears in his eyes. Efrig recited her oath with a fox's smirk while Gunni grinned, guileless with joy. It stirred an acrid longing in my chest.

Though she'd been offered many, Hadhnri had taken no one's love-lock. She couldn't tell them that she kept my own in her pocket, and so people thought her vain, or silly, or childish. Too absorbed with her work. Pedhri Clan Aradoc would set his eye upon her soon, now that Gunni was wed and she to be grown in a few months' time. He wouldn't force her to wed, but he would suspect her reasons, and that would not bode well for me.

When the oaths were spoken and water from the fen was daubed across their heads by Pedhri Clan Aradoc's hand, a loud cheer rose to the roof of the roundhouse. Then there was chaos and laughter as friends of the couples attacked them, unclasping cloaks and whisking away jackets and tugging at belts; as other couples, wed and unwed, found each other and kissed and teased at buttons and clasps; as those who were not participating in the wedding festivities made their laughing exits, chivvying the children out before them. I met Hadhnri's eye across the room, and she nodded subtly. I left while she hung back to steal her brother's cloak.

Outside, the air was apple-sweet and crisp with the Ha'night chill nibbling the edge of summer's last heat. A bonfire kept it from seeping into the bones, and the season's first batch of cider flowed freely. Malgin, a girl a year younger than I, handed me a cup and smiled shyly from beneath thick, dark eyelashes. I took it without thinking, and then she laced her fingers between mine and spun me beneath her hand to the quick-whistle heartbeat of the night.

It might have been innocent. It might have been foolish and bold, as Hadhnri was, in defiance of the unspoken rule—no one had given me a love-lock but Hadhnri. No one but Hadhnri had ever dared show an interest in me. It was startling, and pleasant in its novelty, and I let her lead me around the fire once before I broke our dance with an awkward smile of my own.

I had somewhere to be.

I found Hadhnri standing outside of the roundhouse, wearing her brother's heavy fur cloak jauntily off her shoulder. Her arms were crossed, her eyebrow cocked like her hip.

"Malgin? She never struck me as the kind you favor."

I laughed and glanced back at Malgin, who was dancing someone else around the circle now, her shoulders broad and her steps as certain as Hadhnri's. She was exactly the kind I favored.

"Are you jealous?" I danced around her, my fingers grazing her lower back.

Her stare devoured me. She said simply, in a low voice, "Yes."

Heat rose up my neck to the tips of my ears. "Hurry."

We crept away from the burning light of the fire and beyond our hamlet, into the wild fens. The silence was so sudden, the night so dark, that I thought my ears stopped with mud and my eyes as well. I glanced behind us to make sure no one had followed. Only then did I take Hadhnri's hand in mine.

In the months that had passed since the winter Sunstead, Hadhnri and I had desperately sought a chance to be alone. For a chance to explore beyond the furtive kisses we pressed into each other when we had a moment unchaperoned. We waited for Pedhri Clan Aradoc to leave on clan business, but whenever he went, Gunni stayed, a shit-clod clinging to our boots. At the last Ha'night, as the leaves returned to the trees and fens swelled with rainwater again, we thought Gunni would stay in the roundhouse with Efrig; they'd already shown signs, then. But no. He'd joined us around the fire, goading us into games and drinking the last of the winter's cider until we were all so drunk that Hadhnri and I hadn't a hope of sneaking away.

But not tonight. It was Gunni's wedding night, and Pedhri Clan Aradoc remained in the roundhouse with the rest of the celebrants. My stomach leapt with the thought of it. A lucky thing that Malgin had danced with me. Perhaps people would remember seeing me last with her, and not with Hadhnri.

"Are you sure you don't want to stay in the roundhouse with the rest of them?" Hadhnri asked in the dark. Her voice hid a mischief.

I snorted and shoved her away. The same yearning I'd felt during the oath-making stole over me again, though. What would it be like to share in the tradition of the wedding night, the joyous and unburdened fervor, separate but spurred on by the communal? It would have been harder, much harder, for us to hide, even in the darkness of the roundhouse.

I said, "I want to find the spring again."

She found my hand again in the dark. "Have you been to it since . . ."

I shook my head, realized she might not see it, and murmured, "No. I thought—maybe we would have to be together. Like we were then."

"Do you remember the way?"

"We'll find it."

We walked, trotted occasionally. Hadhnri grew impatient, tugging me back to her for kisses, each one asking more than the last. When we made it to the Baneswood, though, we could not find the spring.

"It's too dark, Agnir."

"We'll find it."

I stopped, bewildered, in a clearing beneath a willow. "It should be here. This is where we found it, isn't it?"

"We were children. Surely we did not run so deep?"

It was difficult to see in the dark, but it was clear there

was no spring. The air was cool, but it was the ordinary coolness of the Ha'night evening, not the frigid cold of that spring. The only sound was the crunch of twig and leaf beneath our boots. Not even squirrel-chatter. It sent a chill up my back.

"Agnir." Hadhnri spun me into her. She kissed me again, drinking me deep, and my whole body tightened with the pleasure of it. "Please. Someone will look for us soon, and if you don't touch me, I will drown myself in the Ene—"

"Don't!" I press her lips closed with my hand. "Do not speak so. Not here. Not even in jest."

She dropped her gaze, chagrined, but it didn't stop her from flitting her tongue out against my fingers and pulling me closer. "Then touch me."

"Ah." I let slip a moan at the flick of her tongue. "Here?"

"By Fate, yes," she breathed against me. "Here, anywhere, so long as you do it now."

How was I to deny what I had desired for so long? I surrendered, and she swept me under in her river-swift rush.

When she and I had our first Making, I thought that was what loving her would be like. The same coming together, the same understanding of where she stopped and where I began and how that line blurred and blurred. This was like that, and it was nothing like that. In the workshop, I didn't think of our bodies beyond the heat of her beside me on the bench. Now I could think of nothing but the fog of her breath against my cheek, of the apple-swell of her breast beneath my hand, the plaintive, wind-sharp keening from her throat.

We were lost, the two of us beneath Gunni's fur cloak. Somewhere, back in the darkness of the clan's roundhouse, other couples made their furtive moves, some silent, some perhaps less than silent, and at the center, the joyous couples and the racket of their lovemaking and the drunken cheers from other pallets as the newly wed cried out. None of that existed for me or Hadhnri. There was us and this moment, alone together in the Baneswood, and though she would not have admitted it, I knew it would be our last, our only. Pedhri Clan Aradoc would not let her have me, no matter how she begged. Not if I begged with her, and I would not. No, he would refuse us, but we would also not be able to hide that we had done this. Someone would have seen us retreat together—and who would we surprise? No one in the clan; all knew Pedhri Clan Aradoc's ward and his daughter were nigh inseparable. Certainly not Pedhri himself.

Knowing this, I buried myself deeper inside her so she would always have a part of me, holding her close in the sweat-dank heat of our clothing until she broke against me.

"Agnir," she murmured against my lips. I shivered in response, resting limp against her until her hand stirred between my legs. She rolled me onto my back, said my name again, and it quickened me—as if I weren't already straining taut. "Sweet Agnir."

"Hadhnri?" It came like a request, but I could not say—exactly—what I was asking for.

She held herself over me on her elbow. Used to the darkness now, I could make out the tenderness around her mouth.

"By my name and my clan, I, Hadhnri Clan Aradoc, pledge myself to you, Agnir Clan Fein," she whispered.

She stole my breath from me with that oath, tonight of all nights—or perhaps with the steadiness of her hand.

I said, chest hitching, "That's three times you've sworn. You will make a spell of this."

"I will," she breathed. "And I will swear again and again if it will keep you by my side."

I bound her to me then, my legs around her hips, my hands around her neck, and in her ear, I whispered, "By my name and my clan, I, Agnir Clan Fein, pledge myself to you, Hadhnri Clan Aradoc."

And so I learned what it was to be unmade by the hands of another.

"We should go back," I whispered sometime later, the sweat on our bodies drying cold.

Hadhnri murmured, love-drunk, from her spot in my neck: "I don't want to go back."

"We'll be missed. Or do you want to live out our days in the Baneswood?"

"Run away with me," she whined. "Are we not wed?"

I smiled against her forehead. "We are wed. But that is our heart-secret, and it will not be a secret if we don't go back now."

Abruptly, Hadhnri stood to riffle through our discarded clothing. Then she returned, shifting from foot to foot, staring down at me, at turns impish and shy, hiding her hands behind her back.

"What?" I lay back on my elbows, smug. "What have you done?"

"I made these for you," she blurted.

Hadhnri thrust two leather bracers into my face. They were tooled in a simple, elegant pattern of knotted bramble. She must have made them without me. I took them carefully.

"I don't have—"

Hadhnri waved my words away. "They're to protect you. As long as I live, no harm will come to you."

I froze. "A Making?" Then I concentrated, and I could feel Hadhnri in it, the way I could in every Making. "You did it alone?"

Hadhnri nodded, her bashfulness returned.

To say I was not frightened would have been a lie. I should have reminded her of her promise. They were beautiful, though, and Hadhnri would never Make malice toward me.

"I love them. Help me put them on."

The Raid

We walked back toward the Aradoc hamlet hand in hand, drunk on pleasure, weaving crooked through the wet grass.

The bonfire had dimmed, no longer a beacon in the night, but the shouting had not faded with it; instead of one single point of light, there were many, erratic and flickering, and the cadence of the cries was wrong.

"Agnir, what's happening?" The bleariness vanished from Hadhnri's voice.

I had never heard brave Hadhnri afraid before.

She began to run, my stubborn Hadhnri, even as my steps faltered.

My body remembered the feel of this moment in a way that my mind could not. I felt the heat of fire licking red-tongued against the black night, smoke choking out the moon, and my father screaming to rally the clan—

"Raid!" Pedhri Clan Aradoc bellowed. He stood outlined against the doorway of the roundhouse, his hips girded in a woven blanket and a sword in his hand. Gunni burst into the night just behind him, dressed in the same fashion, his chest pale and hairless compared to his father's.

Hadhnri pulled up sharp, clutching me close behind her. I thought he would pass us by, but our motion snagged his attention and he slowed. He pointed his bare blade at me.

"Is this your doing, Agnir Ward-Aradoc?"

"No, Father!" Hadhnri cried, placing herself between me and the sword.

"Then explain why Clan Fein has come on the night of your brother's wedding!"

The answer was simple, though fear clamped my throat shut so the words couldn't slide from my mouth. All the clans celebrated their weddings on Ha'nights. Things in common, the rituals of Ha'night and Sunstead. Our shared blood, our shared history, our shared customs. It was not hard to know when and where to plunge the knife.

In his anger, he wouldn't see that. I remembered knuckles like rocks against my jaw. I could form no words, my mouth dry and open with the deer's terror, waiting to be spitted through. Hadhnri held my hand, and even she could not hide her fear.

Later. Later, we both knew, our reckoning would come. But for now, he turned to rally the clan, and the rest took up the cry.

"Raid! Raid!"

While Hadhnri sighed in relief, a light of eagerness in

her eye, I stood paralyzed. Hadhnri took both my hands in hers. "This is not your trueborn home, Agnir Clan Fein, but will you not defend us?"

Will you not defend me, she was asking.

Trembling, I stared at the bracers Hadhnri had given me, remembering her promise. All about us, people were yet shadows, lit against flames as red as memory, and they burned just as bright when I closed my eyes. The enemy howled wolf-sharp to the sliver of the moon as they ran through the hamlet. Gone were the shrill pipes and the wedding drums. The new rhythm of the night was fear and fury.

I thought first of the Queen-Beyond-the-Fens. It had been some time since I saw the men she chose to speak for her, and perhaps she was no longer satisfied sending representatives who returned only with leather pouches and wagons of fuel. Perhaps those were not wergild enough for a murdered man. Perhaps she wanted more.

Then some of the howling resolved itself into words, human speech as raucous as any animal call, and I understood Aradoc-Father's words to me.

"For Clan Fein! For Clan Fein!"

It was like falling through ice. My hands trembled. This was not right. I was made Clan Aradoc's ward so that this *could not happen*. And since it had happened—what would happen to me, now?

Hadhnri looked at me with wide eyes, thinking the same.

Before we could think of a plan, before I could say *This is not my fault*, a man I did not know, who stood as tall and broad as Pedhri Clan Aradoc, marched up to us. Hadhnri placed herself in front of me again. I recalled the oath she made to me in the spring, to protect me, to protect her clan. The bracers. I gripped tight her shoulder, her tunic rough beneath my fingers, so unlike the skin beneath that I had finally traced with my tongue.

"Slave!" The man's face was hidden in shadow and beard, the heaviness of his brow and cheekbone only emphasized by the fire of the torches. Clan Fein's black triangle was tattooed below his right eye. "What is your clan?"

"She is the ward of Pedhri Clan Aradoc, and you will not have her!"

Brave Hadhnri, foolish Hadhnri. She could have been the spit of Bannos the Bold as she wedged herself farther between me and the stranger. His sword gleamed dully in the firelight, though, and it would part her flesh, so butter-soft. I tightened my hand on her shoulder and pulled her back.

"I am Agnir Clan Fein, First-Born Garadin Clan Fein."

The stranger bowed, hand over eye—a salute. "You will come with me, First-Born Garadin Clan Fein."

I did not go. I did not move, legs mired in the bog of my own shock and confusion. I barely breathed.

"You will not have her!" This time, Hadhnri stepped in front of me with her blade ready.

The man slammed his own weapon down on Hadhnri's, and it rang out clear as a cock's call at morning, as clear as Hadhnri's cry as her hand stung and her seax dropped to the earth. With his other hand, he shoved her to the ground. Then he stepped over her, and before I could bring my fists to bear, he picked me up and threw me over his shoulder.

"Hadhnri!" I screamed and kicked as the man turned away with me against his back. He held fast. It was like being held against a tree, deep-rooted and immovable, and I was not an axe. I was not even a dagger.

"Agnir!" Hadhnri was on her hands and knees, struggling to her feet but growing farther and farther away.

"Hadhnri!" I punched and fought and reached for her as she ran after me. I screamed until my captor flung me to the ground. His fist came, hook-curled, and darkness followed.

The Collar

I woke gasping for breath, throbbing pressure in my head, a grip around my throat. I thrashed and flailed with fish-gaped mouth. No second blow sent me back into darkness. Instead, the *shh-shh-shh* in my ear as chains wrapped around my chest and pulled me flat. The more I fought, the tighter the chains gripped, and the less I could breathe—

I stopped fighting.

The chains released me, slowly, and I realized that they were not chains but arms. As my eyes adjusted to the brightness of a roundhouse and the center fire, I recognized the man. The one who had carried me away from Hadhnri as I screamed.

At first, I thought I was in the great Aradoc roundhouse. The same pelts hung from the walls, the same firepit burned in the middle with a pot raised over it, the smoke lingering just enough to scent the room; the same benches, well-worn, the same pallets scattered on the floor with a rack of weapons near to hand. But the chieftain's chair was different, and the people surrounding me were too.

Another man knelt over me, his thousand braids a curtain around us. He gripped my collar tight, held me like I was a rabid-bite hound, the knife in his other hand hovering at my pulse. My throat rolled against his fingers as I swallowed, and my eyes followed the star-keen edge of the blade.

"Agnir, First-Born Garadin Clan Fein?" The man's voice was rough, smoky as burning peat and harsh as spirits. His eyes were deep brown and hooded warily, and a scar curled through his short beard and his thin mustache. His clan tattoo was a faded blue-black triangle pointed down. Fate's Dagger.

"I am Agnir Clan Fein," I said.

The man's face softened and he brushed my cheek with the back of his knuckles. The knife was still in his hands.

"I am Garadin Clan Fein. You are home again. Be welcome."

I held rigid, and a furrow creased deeper the lines of his brow. A strong brow. A proud, crooked nose. A spatter of dark freckles, as if someone had splashed him in the mud flats. He tightened his grip on my collar, and I pulled away automatically.

"It is well," he said, gentle, gentle. "You are not a slave. I will take this off you, my own dear one."

I shivered at the endearment. It felt strange. Pedhri Clan Aradoc had certainly never called me such. How was I to accept it from this stranger claiming to be my father?

And why not? I asked myself. Why could he not be my father? I had seen my face in burnished silver, and perhaps it was not so different.

Garadin Clan Fein pulled harder at my throat.

"Please." My voice, the backhand scrape of metal on bark. "What happened?"

Garadin Clan Fein hesitated and glanced at the Clan Fein members gathered around us. A tight circle, not the full clan. The trusted heads of families, then, or maybe direct relatives. This was not going as he had expected. He eased his fingers from the leather of my collar and sat back on his heels.

The man who called himself Garadin Clan Fein explained how he had ordered a raid to the other side of the fates-bane's forest for one thing and one thing only: First-Born Garadin Clan Fein, the chieftain's child given up for peace.

"Then there will be war?" I croaked.

Garadin Clan Fein flicked his fingers once and, a moment later, water was pressed to my lips. I tried not to think of Hadhnri. Of Pedhri Aradoc-Father. Of Gunni and his new wife. The twins. Everyone was watching me as I walked through a stranger's bog. To ask for their safety—to step false and stick fast—would be a betrayal I couldn't yet understand.

His scar crooked dangerous his smile. "No one was killed." He arched a questioning eyebrow to the man who had taken me. His second, perhaps. The man shook his head and Garadin Clan Fein nodded, satisfied. "It was not that kind of raid. A trespass, but a small one. Clan Fein will take what comes, but I am not worried. I have what I wanted, and Pedhri Clan Aradoc will see he has nothing to gain."

Garadin Clan Fein's fingers twitched toward my collar again.

Unconsciously, I leaned away. "What did you want?"

"You."

The answer did not surprise me, because I had asked the wrong question, again—side-sliding against the truth. I knew I was what he had come for, because I was there, in his roundhouse. He did not strike me as someone to sit jawing easy after failure.

What I really wanted to know was, *Why now?*

"Be still. Let me take this off you."

I knew a command when I heard it. I could not help eyeing Garadin Clan Fein's knuckles. They were bony and hairy, his fingers willow-grace long, but I did not doubt their strength.

I held my eyes shut as the man who called himself my father sawed methodically at the leather collar. The back edge of his steel pressed cold into my throat, jarring me. I stretched my chin far as I could from the point. After an age, I sprang free, toppling backward at the sudden release.

The air was cool against my neck. Tentatively, I touched the naked flesh. Smooth—too smooth—in the center. Calloused along the edges where the leather had rubbed. A crust of dirt and sweat on the outside.

Garadin Fein clenched the cut collar white-knuckled. A tear streaked down his weathered cheekbone.

I remembered the first time Hadhnri had touched my first collar. I remembered how, only earlier tonight, she had traced it with her fingers and then her lips. I wanted to ask for it back.

Instead, I was silent as he stood and dropped it into the center fire.

"Welcome home, Agnir First-Born Garadin Clan Fein."

CLAN
FEIN

The Test

The next afternoon, Clan Fein gawped at what modest gains they had risked their lives and their peace to steal. Garadin Clan Fein led me through them to a patch of sparse grass where a scant handful of scrawny sheep grazed. A small circle of the clan was there, the same who were in the roundhouse last night. In the hazy afternoon light, I could trace the similar patterns of their features, how they mapped close to Garadin Clan Fein.

"You can use a sword?" Garadin Clan Fein said over his shoulder. "Or an axe? Any blade?"

"I can," I said softly.

"Speak up."

"I can, Garadin Clan Fein."

"Which?"

"The seax and the axe. I trained with Pedhri Clan Aradoc's own children."

They appraised me with wolfish eyes, ready to pounce.

I knew I was not much to look at. I was not soft—no one in the Fens was soft—but I'd known from young that I would not be a warrior. Even if Pedhri Clan

Aradoc had been stricter in my training, as strict as he was with Gunni and Hadhnri. I found my skill with the leather and awl a better use for my hands.

Garadin Clan Fein grunted. "Onsgar. Face her. Biudir, give your sister your seax."

At the word "sister," my heart sped. A tall, rangy boy with the same clean brown skin as Garadin Clan Fein walked stork-legged over to me, skinny legs bare beneath his knee-length wrap. He bit both his lips together, but I could see the excitement trying to escape. The twitch at the corners of his eyes gave away his solemnity as he handed me the hilt of his sword.

"Welcome, sister," Biudir said.

I smiled, hesitantly, and Biudir's grin was radiant. He bounded back to our father's side as a second boy approached. Onsgar.

Boy was not . . . quite right. As rangy as Biudir and as dark, Onsgar had a careful furrow to his brow. He couldn't have been older than me; he had no clan mark beneath his eye. He wore his thick black hair in a single large braid plaited close to his scalp.

Onsgar took me by the shoulders, kissed me once on each cheek, and then he also said, "Welcome, sister."

I glanced to Garadin Clan Fein in surprise.

"My children, all together." He gestured wide, first to three women, two in tucked skirts like Biudir's and Garadin Clan Fein's, and one in trousers, all with arms crossed in some degree of distrust or curiosity. "Meet your father-sisters, Agnir. Laudir, Modin, and Hal. We wish to see what you can do."

Onsgar stepped back and drew his own seax. I held Biudir's ready. I tried to ignore the skeptical gaze of my family. I tried to forget my lack of practice, to remember Lughir's chiding in the Aradoc yard. I simply let my body move.

But my body *was* out of practice, and my mind was too loud. I could not *not* remember where I was. I could not *not* look for the thrust Gunni would have made, or anticipate Hadhnri's parry. I could not *not* feel Garadin Clan Fein's gaze, a bore-weevil in my spine.

In the first exchange, Onsgar tripped me, brought the seax jabbing down to linger like a hoverfly over my neck; in the next, he disarmed me, Biudir's blade bouncing to the grass; another and he nudged me gently beneath the arm, between the ribs; again, and he worked into my guard and angled upward to pierce beneath my chin.

"Enough," Garadin Clan Fein called.

Onsgar pulled away immediately. I kept my gaze low as we walked back to the adults. I did not need to see them to feel the disappointment in their silence.

"Raise your eyes, Agnir Clan Fein!" Garadin Fein snapped. "Did I not tell you? You are not a slave."

"Yes, Garadin Clan Fein." I straightened, rigid as a reed switch.

Two of my father-sisters shared a grim look. The shortest one, perhaps a finger's width shorter than me, said, "She's been too long with the farmers. They till and they play and they eat too much. Is she worth the justification we've hand-fed Aradoc by raiding on Ha'night?"

"Peace, Laudir," said Garadin Clan Fein.

My cheeks burned and I stood taller. Set my chin. It was true that Clan Aradoc claimed a substantial part of the richest soil in the fens, and the dry hill the hamlet was built on was large enough for a sizable flock of sheep. No one in Clan Aradoc went hungry, and there was enough to trade away for cowhides and pelts from other clans. Clan Aradoc was not soft, and neither was I. But the reflex of loyalty bit like a blade in my fist and I didn't know what to do with it.

I said, "They didn't soften me beyond use."

Garadin Fein considered the words and considered me. His eyes were dark and probing and this time, I met them, like for like.

"Again, Onsgar, Agnir. Again."

Onsgar saluted his father. I did not. We fought again. This time, Garadin Clan Fein did not stop us until I had disarmed Onsgar and wrestled him to the ground, my own weapon discarded in favor of my fingers, swiping falcon-clawed at his eyes.

Garadin Fein came, unhurried, to stand above us. I looked up, chest heaving. Blood trickled from Onsgar's lip down his chin.

"You yet have Clan Fein's iron in you. Good." The chieftain offered me his hand.

That night Garadin Clan Fein and my father-sisters welcomed me with a feast so that the clan would know me. Instead of lamb turning over the fires, we ate beef from one of the precious cattle that Clan Fein raised in the damp lowlands. It was hot and smoky and dripping with grease. There was song, with more drumming and stamping than Aradoc's whistling bird-melody, but it thrummed its way into the rhythm of my own heart's beat, sliding into the gaps where something had been missing all my life. Something I'd been near enough to feel the heat of, but never close enough to grow warm in.

Well into the night, I was called to the chieftain's seat. As I marched up to Garadin Clan Fein—and all through the night, besides—I imagined the clan's eyes on me, suspicious and wary, perhaps not so convinced of me as this man with his proud eagle stare.

Garadin Fein gave no sign that he shared their fears. Though it was not Sunstead, he bade me kneel before him. I gave him my oath to Clan Fein before one and all, and I was tattooed at his feet with a triangle beneath my right eye. Clan Aradoc could not claim me now, even if they wanted, and in that way, I was safe. It was a binding, as sure and tight as my collar.

That night, as I lay on my pallet in the great

roundhouse—inhaling the heavy leather-and-oil scent of my bracers, the smell that reminded me of home, of Hadhnri—my mind settled on the one small thing it could contain: I was an adult before Hadhnri. I was older than her and oh, how angry she would be. It made me smile. It made me weep, and my new mark stung.

The Tale Goes like This

Bannos the Bold killed the fates-bane.

Bannos the Clever trapped the fates-bane in a cage of briars.

Bannos the Bold stole the fates-bane's child.

Bannos the Clever tricked the fates-bane from the Fens.

And how did Bannos the Clever, Bannos the Bold defeat the fates-bane? How did he turn his ill-luck to the fates-bane's own doom?

Before the twig could crack beneath his boots, before the frog could startle his prey, Bannos the Clever strung chimes throughout the trees, and when the fen winds blew, their noise was the birdsong of a hundred hundred starlings. No other noise could be heard beneath it.

He carved out his own eye and threw it at the fates-bane's feet, and his arrow pierced it in the throat while it bent over the gift.

Before his hilt could fall apart, Bannos the Bold held his sword high over the luck-hound, so that the blade plunged, falcon-dive upon its breast.

Bannos the Clever could make anything grow.
Bannos the Bold had no mercy in his heart.
Bannos the Clever had a tongue like honey.
Bannos the Bold kept his clan safe from the dark.

The Plan

I found my place in Clan Fein among the crafters. Garadin Clan Fein paired me with Yordi, the squint-eyed tanner with a constant sneer from the smell. It took some time for the woman's hands to catch the intricacies of my designs, and she complained at first—they were impossible, too complicated, a waste of her time. We compromised. She resisted less and I simplified my plans, or I tooled the more complicated bits myself. I was content with the pieces, but they were nothing like the work Hadhnri and I did together.

I never tried to do a Making without Hadhnri. It ached too much to think of it, that feeling coming over me without her there.

Days passed. Weeks. Months. Seasons. A full year and I never stopped thinking of the gentle surety of her fingers. On leather. On my collar. On my skin. I wore her bracers even when I slept, as much to be close to her as for the protection she swore would be mine so long as she lived.

After another year, though, and another, time swept

in like the rivers, burying the peat of my memory deeper and packing it tight. One young woman offered me a love-lock. Solwin, the blacksmith's apprentice. We shared company for a time, after I'd reconciled myself to never returning to Clan Aradoc and accepted the likelihood that Hadhnri had been made to move on by Pedhri Clan Aradoc. It was a selfish solace, though, for I refused the lock, and eventually, Solwin ceased to seek me out. I wondered, briefly, how much of her attentions had been another attempt to keep me hound-bound at Clan Fein's heel. It mattered not; I was part of Clan Fein now, part of its rhythms. I had learned its twining relationships, its moods, its petty rivalries as well as I'd known Clan Aradoc's. Maybe I would never see Hadhnri again. I started to reconsider the blacksmith's love-lock.

And then, one day near first Ha'night, when the flies were buzzing over the lowlands and the geese had returned from their southern winter, Garadin Clan Fein called me into the roundhouse while he was meeting with my father-sisters and his other advisers. Dhorfnir, the man who had found me during the raid, sat beside my father, picking his teeth with a reed. He hailed me with a grin, raising his hand, great as a wolfhound's paw.

I had never been invited to a meeting of Pedhri Clan Aradoc and his advisers. I stood straighter as I joined my father. I was only a craftsman, but my cloak sat well over the breadth of my shoulders.

"Come, Agnir First-Born. We need your guidance."

Garadin Clan Fein poured me sweet apple mead and sat me on the bench beside him. His eyes crinkled with affection. His clan tattoo matched mine, though it was faded, bleeding soft at the edges where his skin had slackened.

I laughed, uncertain what guidance I could offer. Probably the prices our traders should ask for my next batch of leatherwork. "On my name and my clan, it is yours." I covered an eye with one hand.

No one else laughed, not even Dhorfnir.

I paused with my cup at my lips. "What do you need?"

"What do you know of Pedhri Clan Aradoc's plans for the Fens?" my father asked.

I froze rabbit-still, sighted by the hawk. "Nothing. Pedhri Clan Aradoc did not think me worth his confidences."

Garadin Fein cocked one hand on his skirted thigh and stared into his cup. "You were there a long time, Agnir First-Born. You're observant and careful. What did you see? What did you hear?"

"Tell us any small thing," Modin, my eldest father-sister, said. "We'll fit it where it belongs."

The only secret I knew was my own, mine and Hadhnri's. Did I dare tell him what she and I had done together? Hadhnri said she had done a Making on my own bracers, alone. Could I too?

I looked from one Fein to another, stroking the bracers. A nervous habit, these last years. Garadin Clan Fein's glance dropped to them and I stopped.

"What is it you want to do?" I asked.

My father considered me, and considered again. The clan mark beneath my eye burned coal-bright with the weight of his regard.

"There will be a clan moot at Sunstead next. We are making a plan."

I stopped breathing.

And how would my father's regard fall, if I confessed? What would Clan Fein see when they looked at me? Would I still belong to Clan Aradoc, or would I finally be wholly theirs?

I had been silent too long. I spoke the first thing that came to my lips.

"Pedhri Clan Aradoc takes gifts from the Queen-Beyond-the-Fens." The tale that spilled forth was not a lie, but I spoke with more certainty than my knowledge deserved. "And he sends gifts back. Many were the work of my own hand. Someday, someone from Clan Aradoc will marry into her family, and he will cede some of the Fens to her."

Anxious glances, angry glances passed between my father's council. Garadin Clan Fein's face tightened—at the eyes, the lips, the nose, a great narrowing like a wary feline.

"What lands does he plan to cede to her?" he asked me.

"Does it matter?" said Laudir, the middle father-sister. "We will not let him barter clan land away. He will have to kill us to the last before he pries it from our fingers."

"The better question is this," said Modin-father-sister. "What will she do with them?"

"She will drain the fens to get to the peat," said Hal-father-sister, the youngest. "Then they will plant, and where they cannot plant, they will build roads from her lands to the coast, and at the coast, ships. That is what she wants."

I glanced sharply to Hal. "Drain the fens?"

With a pulsing ache, my thoughts flew swift to the lowlands where I had caught leaping frogs, tickled fish against my palms, watched the herons and their elegant steps. Where would they go? I felt the wrench of the loss and I had not even lost it yet.

Or perhaps I had. I had lost the home I knew once, and then once again. Could I bear it a third time, this time to a strange woman of gold and dye who did not love the Fens as I did?

"How could he do something like that?" I asked.

Laudir-father-sister laughed at me and its bite was unkind. "You are naive, little frog. What would a man not do for power? Even Bannos the Bold was tempted."

I ducked my gaze and stared at my own hands, brown and smooth but for a few childhood scars.

"Thank you, Agnir. You may go." Garadin Clan Fein's dismissal was polite but firm. "We will raise this at the moot."

I stood and saluted, bowing while covering my unmarked eye. "Whatever you need, Father." I started to go, but my chest throbbed with a different ache. I turned back to him, to them, all of them waiting for me to leave so that they might speak their secrets. "I have—had a friend. Hadhnri Second-Born Pedhri Clan Aradoc. She would be an ally. I know it."

Laudir-father-sister sucked her teeth.

Garadin Clan Fein simply said again, "Thank you, Agnir."

The Road

Shortly after Ha'night, I accompanied Dhorfnir and Solwin and a few others to trade with Clan Hanarin. We traveled east and north, keeping the Baneswood to our left as we walked, one temperamental donkey to carry the load. Clan Fein was largely isolated from the other clans, cut off by the darkness of the wood. It made for a journey of days instead of hours.

I had prepared our leather goods, belts and boots and also a thick jerkin for Erci Clan Hanarin, their chieftain. I'd tooled it with running wolves and leaping hinds, though I could not but remember the wolf at the herald's man's throat. I tried to reassure myself: There was nothing of the Making in this work.

For all that Solwin and I were sometimes awkward around each other, it was a pleasant journey. Dhorfnir told stories of Bannos the Bold in his deep, rumbling chant, and Solwin sang in the hauntingly high voice that seemed incongruous with her thick-corded arms.

When we camped, we set watches, but instead of watching the road for raiders, Dhorfnir bade us keep just as close a watch upon the Baneswood, with its willowy shadows, deep pockets of dark between the trees.

The first night, when it was my turn, I sat cross-legged just beyond the ring of the low fire's warmth. The seax Fein-Father had given me—the blade Aradoc-Father had refused me—was cradled in my lap. I stroked the leather of my bracers to ease my nerves and stared into the wood.

A chill shivered up my spine, but I felt it whenever I was this near the Baneswood—which was often, because Clan Fein's meager allotment of the fens abutted its southern edge. The shiver wasn't the fear-chill that overtook other members of Clan Fein, who called up quick luck by covering their unmarked eye or thumbed a torc or a pocketed love-lock. It was like something called to me, too high-pitched to be heard by anyone else. Sometimes, I imagined it was Hadhnri, standing on the other side, thinking of me.

Other times, though, I was certain it was the fatesbane, calling to the curse it had laid upon us.

"Agnir!" Dhorfnir barked, shaking me roughly. "You tempt the luck-hound."

I jerked out of my reverie to find that I was standing, my wool blanket hanging limply from one shoulder. This must not have been the first time he had called my name. I drew the blanket back around both shoulders and pulled my focus away from the Baneswood.

The large man stared into my eyes, looking me up and down. "What did you see, little frog?"

"Nothing." I turned back to the woods. They were dark, forbidding, but they were only trees. The dog-whistle call that tightened my heart was gone, like the broken thread of a spider's web.

He narrowed his eyes at me and guided me back to the fire.

"I'll finish my watch," I protested, but he ignored me and nudged Solwin awake with his boot.

"Watch," he grunted.

Solwin looked to me, then to the sky above, still dark and star-speckled.

"It's not my turn yet." She slumped back beneath her blanket and covered her head.

"I can—" I started.

Dhorfnir jostled Solwin harder. "Watch!"

"Hie!" she yelped and jumped up with her blankets, near rolling into the fire. She scowled at the two of us as she stood. There was hint of question in her eye, but she kept it to herself and stomped away.

I took her bedroll and stole comfort from the warmth she'd left behind. I felt eyes on me even in my dreams—Dhorfnir's or another's, I couldn't say.

He didn't let me take another watch alone.

Clan Hanarin was situated on a small island in the middle of the wetlands at the head of a rivulet. They were a small clan, and their holdings smaller even than Clan Fein's, though their land was better. They welcomed us with warm drinks, and we presented Erci Clan Hanarin with the jerkin I'd made. The chieftain eyed me carefully after my introduction as Agnir First-Born Garadin Clan Fein. She studied the jerkin with pursed lips, testing the thickness with her calloused thumbs. She and Dhorfnir stared in wordless exchange, but that was clearly not enough, because Erci took Dhorfnir aside. I stared after them until Solwin prodded me roughly, nodding toward the donkey and the clan members waiting to do business with us.

My leatherwork sold well, though I gave the bartering no more than half a mind. I saw this journey with new eyes. The jerkin I had made—it was not a gift for the sake of its fineness, as I had obliviously thought. It was armor. A gift for battle. Dhorfnir was here to recruit Erci Clan Hanarin to my father's side against Clan Aradoc, to tell her of Pedhri Clan Aradoc's intent to parcel the Fens away—which I had relayed to him.

I tried to soothe the thought. Fein-Father said they would discuss it at the clan moot. There need not be fighting if Garadin Clan Fein could unite enough of the clans, or if Pedhri Clan Aradoc saw sense. Unease set my stomach to a low boil.

I suddenly missed Making with Hadhnri, and not, for once, because I missed feeling close to her. I missed our Makings because she had been right: when we Made things, I felt as if I had the power to change the world. To bend it, even a little, to my will. I stared at the belts draped over my knees, tracing with my eyes the dancing trout I had worked. I longed for that feeling again. I clenched my fingers tight so that my nails dug into my palm.

I would not call the fates-bane's eye upon me again.

"Are you well, Agnir?" Solwin peered into my face with suspicious concern.

"Fine," I snapped.

Her face flushed red. She turned back to her buckles and tools and to the man of Clan Hanarin admiring her silverwork. She was a fine smith, and a fine woman, just the kind I favored, as Hadhnri would put it. More importantly, she was a friend, whatever else had gone between us.

"I'm sorry," I mumbled after the man had gone to fetch whatever Solwin wanted in trade. "All this talk of Clan Aradoc. It makes me uneasy to think of war between the clans."

Solwin eyed me from the side. I waited for her to question my loyalty to Clan Fein.

Instead, she asked, looking down at her silver and iron, "Why did Dhorfnir take you off watch?"

The question caught me off guard. With no need to feign the embarrassment warming my face, I stumbled, "He—um. Caught me sleeping. Said he'd tell my father." A damning lie, but it was better than the cursed truth, that the Baneswood had called to me and I longed to answer.

Solwin raised a skeptical eyebrow and grunted.

After that, our conversation came in drought-trickles. Dhorfnir also grew odd with me. On our journey back to Clan Fein, he stayed close to me, as if I were a sheep and he my shepherd. I would have been annoyed if the Baneswood weren't calling out to me again, stronger this time. I kept drifting unconsciously from the path, and each time he urged me back with a gentle nudge, or a word to pull my attention. His heavy brow was furrowed with concern.

Once, he had to yank me back, nearly jerking my shoulder out of its socket.

"Into the water, is it, little frog?" he laughed.

I looked to my footing. I was one step from falling into the bog.

"Over here," he murmured, not unkindly, moving to stand between me and the wood. He put the donkey between us to make an even greater wall between myself and the Baneswood's call. The luck-hound's call.

It worked. We walked on like that for the rest of the first day and all the next, and that spider silk tether that tugged my gaze west weakened. I laughed to think I needed to be blindered like the donkey.

After, I wondered if what happened next was my fault—if the fates-bane took my laughter for defiance.

FATE'S BANE

We were walking and eating strips of smoked fish the next day when a heron burst up from the rushes, winging its way across our path, startling us all, even the donkey. It jerked and shoved either way, knocking into my shoulder and throwing Dhorfnir off-balance. Then, louder than the donkey's braying came Dhorfnir's scream of pain.

While someone grabbed at the beast's halter, I ran around it to see Dhorfnir knee-deep in fenswater. I thought the worst—a broken leg.

"Solwin," I called, "help me!"

She was already there, along with another of the men. Dhorfnir was a heavy man and he groaned through his teeth as we raised him out of the morass and set him on solid ground.

I took my seax and cut the leg of his trousers to see the break, only to find that, despite the blood, the bone felt whole.

"There," Solwin grunted. She pointed to a puncture in Dhorfnir's calf, half as long as finger.

I frowned, confused, but Solwin was already back at the spot where Dhorfnir had fallen, fishing gingerly in the puddle with her hand. Carefully, she pulled out a broken seax. It dripped with dark water, pitted and filthy.

Dhorfnir saw it as she brought it over and his face settled in resignation. "By the fates-bane's tears."

"You'll be all right," Solwin murmured. "Come on. Agnir, unload that stupid animal. Dhorfnir, you'll ride. We'll get you to Rodhi, and she'll make you right."

She had the sound of someone trying to convince herself. I couldn't muster any words at all. I did as she said. Dhorfnir sagged on the donkey's back but grimaced a smile when he saw my face.

"It's all right, little frog," he said.

Dhorfnir caught fever before we reached home.

Garadin Clan Fein was at his side when the fever took him. There was nothing our healer could do.

From that day on, my father's temper sharpened. The clan feared to cross him, but there was even more swearing at the luck-hound, and worse—half whispers that the joining of the clans was cursed by the fates-bane, and that we would do better to let Aradoc have his way.

Only once did someone dare say I had brought the ill-luck upon them all.

"My heart has stopped because of you!" Thimar, Dhorfnir's wife, spat at my feet as I was leaving the roundhouse.

Garadin Clan Fein was there in a breath. He didn't say a word, but Thimar shrank away, and no one confronted me again. From that moment, though, I could see the doubt in my father's eyes. The hollow ache of their silent questioning never left me.

I knew then what I was to my father. Why he claimed me when he did, why he would allow no accusations of ill-luck to smirch me. I was a symbol to him and all those he called to him—in taking me as ward, Pedhri Clan Aradoc had wounded him, but Garadin Clan Fein had struck back. Without me as hostage, Aradoc was no longer immune to Fein's wrath. My father could make the war he wished.

The war I told Hadhnri would never come.

The Clan Moot

Sunstead next brought the clan moot, and I spent the months in between Ha'night and Sunstead giddy with the possibility of seeing Hadhnri and terrified of the foot-snag currents flowing between the clans.

Members of the other clans who I had first met as Ward Pedhri Clan Aradoc came to visit Garadin Clan Fein's roundhouse. They ate at his fire, drank his mead, and departed in the night. They looked hard at me before they left. They'd all sat kitten-meek under Pedhri Clan Aradoc after he defeated Clan Fein, but now their discontent shifted like silt underfoot.

With the Sunstead sun hanging at its zenith, we gathered in the land of Clan Pall to discuss the fate of the Fens. I arrived with my father and Onsgar and our elder and middle father-sisters. We of Clan Fein were a rangy lot. My father had been right; the Aradoc bounty did soften them. I looked for a glimpse of that softness in the crowd of other clans, but I could find Hadhnri nowhere—just once the back of a head, broad, cloaked shoulders, and a particular walk.

"You're not looking for an Aradoc girl, are you?" Onsgar said, catching my glances. He had a sharp eye and sharper elbows.

I nudged him in his own ribs. In the last few years, he'd grown taller than me, and I'd grown fond of him. It was a different thing, to have younger brothers. It lessened the sting of losing Hadhnri and Gunni and sharpened it in the same bite.

"Mind your own beard," I muttered as we found our places in the center round outside the roundhouse. Onsgar scratched his pitiful chin hairs protectively.

Beneath the bright sun, surrounded by their picked men and women, the clan leaders bickered back and forth over what was to be done with the Fens, and who was closest in the lineage to Bannos the Clever, Bannos the Bold, and thus had claim to what land.

My father sat quiet on the wooden bench until he did not. When he stood, the other clan chiefs stepped back as if this were a signal long awaited. All save Pedhri Clan Aradoc, but he, too, looked as if he'd expected this moment.

"I am Garadin Clan Fein. By my name and my clan, I pledge myself to the keeping of the Fens and their people." My father's voice was deep and clear, and it carried above the round where we all of us sat, silent. "To their fish and their fowl. To their beasts and their burdens. That is the oath that I made when I became chieftain of Clan Fein. It's the oath we expect of our leaders. Is this not so?" The chieftains near him nodded, but that was not enough for my father. He spun to us on the benches, his braids swinging, his arms held out like a tale-teller. "Is this not the oath Bannos the Bold himself spoke when he became chief of all the Fens?"

This time, the agreement was loud and it came from all quarters. Pedhri Clan Aradoc looked ready to speak, but my father spoke smoothly into the space he'd left himself.

"These are the oaths anyone calling themselves the chief of chiefs should hold true above all, and yet." My father turned a cold, dark eye, disappointed and grim, on my foster father. "Pedhri Clan Aradoc plots to give away our land and our peace to a woman who calls herself queen. A woman who would take our land and have us kneel to her, while her god's heralds take our gold and their soldiers take our youths for bed slaves. Is that how we keep the Fens and their people?"

The heavy pit in my stomach grew large as a stone and just as solid. This was what I had given my father. I had done this, had helped sow this rift between the clans. I could only wish that the words would be enough.

"What would you know of peace, truce-breaker?" Pedhri Clan Aradoc turned against my father. His voice was a deep, threatening rumble that seemed to come from the earth below. "You broke the peace on a Ha'night! My own child's wedding. Does that honor the Fens?"

What will happen to me, if Clan Fein attacks Clan

Aradoc? I had asked Hadhnri in the halcyon beauty of the Baneswood spring. I had scented the blood in the air even then, sure as a hound.

I could smell it now.

"No one was hurt in that raid, and nothing was taken but what belonged already to me."

The eyes of every chieftain turned toward me. Even Pedhri Clan Aradoc's. I tried to imagine what he saw. I was different now. Taller, my hair in the numerous Fein braids though cut close to the scalp at my temples. The blue-black triangle below my right eye. The scar-like line about my throat that had not faded.

He looked at me as he never had when I was his ward. I was less than his charge, less even than a slave, and yet I felt as if he truly saw me for the first time. He saw an enemy.

My face heated, but I knew I could not look away. Beside me, Onsgar sat straight-backed and proud, and his presence gave me strength.

As Garadin Clan Fein's inked, bare chest swelled proud against Pedhri Clan Aradoc in the high sun, I saw her. Hadhnri Second-Born Pedhri Clan Aradoc. In the sunlight, her curls sparked more red than brown. She was taller than I remembered, her shoulders thicker with muscle in her sleeveless tunic and leather jerkin, silver rings around the meat of her arm. She stared at me with all the rest, truer than an arrow and cold as iron. She turned away.

No matter how I begged in my heart, she did not look again.

The attention of the clans returned to the chiefs, and when Hadhnri left the close pack of Clan Aradoc, I rose to follow. Onsgar raised one dark eyebrow.

"Father will not like to know you've met Second-Born Pedhri Clan Aradoc in secret, sister."

"Then you will not tell him, brother. Besides"—I jerked my head at the busy round and the busy village beyond, where the rest of Clan Pall was readying the evening's feast and games—"no meeting here can be a secret."

That was the point of a clan moot, after all; all secrets came to light at a moot.

He caught my arm. "Is she the reason you never gave Solwin a love-lock?"

My mouth flattened to a tight line. So did Onsgar's. He released me without a word.

I caught up to Hadhnri at the piss ditches.

"Hadhnri!" I called, trying and failing to restrain my eagerness. "It's me, Agnir." As if she could not recognize me, the way I had recognized her—in an instant.

Hadhnri turned to me and I stopped short. She had lost some of the softness in her cheeks—only some—but it made the hard clench of her jaw stand out. The Aradoc mark, Fate's Crossroads, stood starkly pale in thick, cross-hatched scars beneath her right eye.

"You dare speak to me, Agnir First-Born Garadin Clan Fein?"

The first time I heard my name from her lips in years, and she spat it so hatefully that it burned. She could not have wounded me more with the seax at her hip.

She marched at me and yet I stood, frozen. "My father took you in and treated you as his own. He honored you with a place at his table and trusted you with the words spoken there, instead of banishing you like a dog outside. You repaid him by telling those secrets to Garadin Clan Fein?"

My outstretched hands hung like broken reeds.

Hadhnri shut her eyes briefly, then muttered, "I never believed him when he said all of Clan Fein were cunning as adders. Not you, I said. Never you. I should have listened."

"I didn't know this is what he wanted," I lied.

"Then you are a fool, Agnir. Is there no loyalty in you at all? To me, if not to my clan?"

But even as she glared at me, even as my heart ached, my own fury built.

"You still don't understand, do you, Hadhnri?" I hissed. "You've never wanted for a thing in your life. The love of your father is certain, your place in the clan fast. You can afford to throw that away. I could not. I *can*not. Not even for love."

It was like the days she begged me to run away with her as children, our love-locks a tight-clutched secret.

Hadhnri bit her lower lip and inhaled sharply. The silence grew until I did not know what could fill the chasm between us. Finally, she took a shuddering breath. "I couldn't wait to see you today."

My breath caught but I held back my tears. I couldn't say which disgusted her more—my betrayal or her own naivety. She turned her back to me.

"Hadhnri, wait!" I called. Hadhnri looked over her shoulder and I held up the bracers she had Made for me. "I still wear them."

Her gaze softened like wax and hardened again just as quick.

"You are not the girl I made them for."

The Attack

"Did it not go well with your Aradoc girl?" Onsgar whispered when I rejoined the moot alone.

I glared balefully up at him, and the kicked-dog look of me hushed any jokes at my expense. I was glad it was just him to contend with and not Biudir as well. Biudir was clever for his age but lacked the wisdom of silence.

When Hadhnri rejoined her clan, I tried not to look at her. I felt rotted through, and I watched Pedhri Clan Aradoc with a new hatred that grew out of that rotten center.

The sun had begun its descent when Lidwul Clan Pall, host of the moot, called a stop to the discussions. The smell of roasting meat and baking bread had grown strong as the day stretched on; it was a relief to mask the tensions in food and drink, to trade boasting over clan lineage to the simple boasting of strength and skill. I cheered on Laudir-father-sister as she wrestled Soli Clan Elyin's wife, and Modin-father-sister as she drank Erci Clan Hanarin to the ground. There was music and dancing in the thick green grass. There was Aradoc mutton, steamed fish, and baked fowl, and I ate to bursting. I could almost ignore the way Hadhnri and the rest of Clan Aradoc avoided me.

Then, with the sun low enough to bleed the sky, came the most important part of the moot: the exchanging of gifts between the clans. Fine weapons and leather goods, worked pelts and beautiful weaves, torcs and bands and buckles of gold and silver.

It all felt as hollow as my own chest. I went to bed early and let others keep the pretense of peace.

I woke on my pallet on the warm ground to an inhuman scream, my heart pounding in my ears. I waited for the fox-cry to come again, but the next sound was all-too-human: a roar of outrage that I recognized.

"Garadin Fein!" That familiar fury echoed through the starry night. "Come and face me, Garadin Clan Fein!"

Clan Fein roused around me and I heard in the distance the other clans rising to investigate the sounds coming from the area where Clan Aradoc had made their beds. My eyes adjusted as I followed my father to where Pedhri Clan Aradoc stood, flanked by Gunni and Lughir the weaponmaster. Hadhnri stood behind her brother, arms crossed just like his. They were a thick, broad family, standing like bears before my father, and I could see why they had claimed so much of the Fens.

"You slink like a coward in the night, Garadin Fein,

yet you've nerve to claim Bannos the Bold as your line?" Pedhri Clan Aradoc spat at my father's bare feet.

Laudir-father-sister bristled, but my father held her back with an open hand.

"What happened here?" Garadin Clan Fein asked, his voice low and calm. He crossed his arms over his own bare chest.

"You claim ignorance?" Pedhri Clan Aradoc stepped forward. "When this was found by my own son's head?"

I checked my gasp as he held out a dagger in a beautiful sheath. I recognized it from the day's gift-giving. It had been a gift to Clan Fein from Clan Aradoc, and I'd known the work immediately for Hadhnri's. A deepening in the crease between his brows was the only sign my father gave. A silent look passed between him and Modin-father-sister as he took it.

"You claim an attempt on your son's life, but where is the would-be murderer?" Fein-Father asked.

"Run away like a coward when I woke," Gunni Clan Aradoc said. He spoke with a man's voice now.

"Then you cannot insist it was Clan Fein to break the moot peace."

"Only Clan Fein was given this blade, this sheath." Pedhri Clan Aradoc looked to the clan leaders gathered about them. "Clan Aradoc demands payment for this offense."

Suspicion tickled the back of my neck and I looked to Hadhnri, who would not meet my gaze.

Fein-Father scoffed. "I will not forfeit one of mine for an Aradoc trick."

"You have forfeited your own before," Aradoc-Father said. His regard swallowed me whole. "Left her like a snake at my breast, to poison my own heart against me."

"You will watch your tongue, Aradoc, or I will cut it out!" Garadin Clan Fein snarled, unsheathing that fatal gift-dagger.

That same shriek echoed through the night, this time with all in witness. My father stared at the blade as if it were adder-fanged. Then I understood. I shoved between my father and father-sisters and took the blade from his hand, slamming it home into the sheath. The monstrous noise went silent. In my hand, I felt a certainty that I hadn't felt in years.

This time, I found Hadhnri's eyes and held them.

Lidwul Clan Pall came to stand between the leaders of Aradoc and Fein. He looked apologetically at my father before saying, "It is my clan's honor to maintain the peace on our lands during the moot. Were any hurt?"

Pedhri Clan Aradoc shook his head.

"Did you order your clan to attack in the night?" Lidwul Clan Pall asked my father.

Garadin Clan Fein shook his head.

"Then all is well. For the sake of the peace, though, we will have a duel tomorrow. Let strength and wit decide this matter." Lidwul Clan Pall pulled Garadin Clan

Fein and Pedhri Clan Aradoc each by the hand and bade them clasp arms.

I did not see what disdain or hatred was stoked between my father and my foster as they gripped each other, for I was yet gripped by Hadhnri's stare and the accusation graven there.

The Duel

"Let me take this duel, brother," murmured Modin-father-sister as Garadin Clan Fein stormed back to our pallets. "I will right this."

I stopped in my tracks and my middle father-sister bumped into me in the darkness. Laudir-father-sister caught herself, and then gave my shoulders a rough squeeze.

"Did you order this, Father?"

My father half turned to look at me over his shoulder. His eyes rose to Laudir, behind me. She squeezed my shoulders tighter, fingernails digging into my naked skin, then shoved me forward. I followed like a gosling behind them, clutching the dagger in my hand, tingling from Hadhnri's presence in the Making.

"Who will he send to fight for Clan Aradoc?" Laudir asked.

"Gunni First-Born Pedhri Clan Aradoc," I spoke up without thinking. If Pedhri did not suggest it, Gunni would demand the chance to prove himself before all the clans. The next words—what I knew of Gunni's strengths and weaknesses, his fighting style—burned away like mist under the blaze of a memory:

Is there no loyalty in you at all? To me, if not to my clan?

There I stood, caught between Hadhnri's scorn and my father's reservation, his dark eyes gleaming in the starlight. As he weighed me, I held my chin up. I had learned that much, in the years since I stopped wearing a collar.

"Then I must send one of my own children."

Now, I bowed my head. I was no match for Gunni, but he was First-Born Clan Aradoc, and I was First-Born Clan Fein.

"I will stand for Clan Fein."

Garadin Clan Fein continued to stare at me, and when he spoke, it was not without affection. "I will send Onsgar."

Relief and disappointment split me in half. Perhaps Onsgar had told our father about Hadhnri. I did not want to duel Gunni and was glad to have the choice taken from me, but I could not bear to be deemed unfaithful by someone else I thought I loved. To be pushed beyond the borders of the light and warmth of a clan every time I came too close.

"Do you not trust me, Father? I will fight him for you."

My father draped a wiry arm around my shoulder and steered us onward to our pallets while my father-sisters trailed alongside.

"Fear not, my child. I know you are mine. The adder

at his breast." He snorted. "Come. You will tell Onsgar what you know of Gunni First-Born Pedhri Clan Aradoc."

So I told him all that I knew, and the next morning, the clans circled about Onsgar and Gunni, one my trueborn brother whom I'd known only a few years, and one my foster brother, whom I'd known as long as I could remember. They were of a height, though Gunni was older by a handspan and clearly had strength on his side. Onsgar had speed, though, and he was clever as Bannos. The steel of their swords shone bright as the Sunstead sun. Our fathers stood on the edge of the circle behind each son, pretending they did not fear.

But I feared, and I stood beside Hadhnri, halfway along the circle between our fathers.

"This is your fault," I whispered to her. "That sheath was a Making. You *promised me*—"

"*I* did not pull that dagger, Agnir," Hadhnri said. "If you Fein weren't planning betrayal all along, how did this happen?"

"No one in Clan Fein has claimed the attack." Though I knew the truth, and it thickened my throat.

"Then Clan Fein are liars and cowards both."

I turned on her in rage, then, tearing my eyes away from our brothers. I wanted to shout, but I could not look at her without seeing the girl she once was, kissing me in the spring and giving me her oath. Pain stole my breath, and all I could do was whisper.

"Do not speak of my family so, Hadhnri."

The rebuke silenced her and we turned at Lidwul Clan Pall's shout. The duel had begun.

Relief that my father did not choose me grew with each exchange. More than one warrior had been maimed for the good of their clan's honor or their own. More than one had died. Though Garadin Clan Fein made me keep closer to the blade than Pedhri Clan Aradoc, I was no prodigy, not so strong as Gunni, nor so quick as Onsgar.

There was a wind that morning, and it rose the hair upon my bare arms. I thought of the wind in Bannos's chimes, and hoped it was a sign of his favor.

Hadhnri's breathing slipped. "Are those—your bracers."

I nodded grimly. If I could not wear them in battle, then Onsgar would, and may the luck-hound protect him.

"I made those for you."

"I thought I was not the girl you made them for?"

We held our breath as Gunni's mighty downward blow made to cleave Onsgar's head like a harvestide squash, but Onsgar slipped around, his own blade darting under Gunni's arm. Gunni spun his blade back in time to knock it away, and they reset again.

I twitched to reach for Hadhnri's hand, clenched tight at her side. I folded my arms across my chest instead.

Hadhnri gasped each time Onsgar's blade came near to Gunni, and it echoed in me. I hated myself for it. But how was I meant to forget wrestling with Gunni outside of the Aradoc roundhouse? It was as clear to me as my memory of fighting Onsgar for the first time: of all of Clan Fein, Onsgar had accepted me first and most readily.

Sister, they both called me.

The end came swiftly. I leapt forward as Onsgar slammed into the ground. I heard the breath rush out of him. Hadhnri grabbed my arm, holding me back.

"Do you, Onsgar Second-Born Garadin Clan Fein, yield to me, Gunni First-Born Pedhri Clan Aradoc?" Gunni's voice was low and clear.

I held myself tense in Hadhnri's grip, no longer fighting her but not easy in her embrace.

"Yield," I begged Onsgar under my breath. Clan Fein had surrendered once to Clan Aradoc to bide its time; I was proof of that. "Yield."

Hadhnri's fingernails dug into the flesh of my naked forearms, and I sank into that pain. Onsgar opened his mouth and I stopped breathing to hear his words. We all did. And so, when he swept Gunni's legs from beneath him, sending the bigger man down, the only sound was our great intake of air as our hearts began to beat again.

My brothers scrambled to their feet, reclaimed their weapons, and circled each other anew. The energy was different now, the outcome no longer sure. The wind itself seemed riled, cool against my sweating skin, buoying the mounting tension as we watched. One exchange, another. Modin-father-sister paced behind my father, while

Laudir-father-sister was so like a boulder she could have grown moss. If only the fight would last long enough.

That was the only hope I had now, for both brothers to survive.

Hadhnri did not let go my arm.

I wished, then, that I had never been taken in the raid—not the first raid, from Clan Fein, but the second, from Clan Aradoc. I wished that I was still Agnir Ward-Aradoc and that I had stayed at Hadhnri's side. That I had never gotten to know Onsgar or Garadin Clan Fein. With my life, I had bought peace. And I had never felt so trapped as I did now.

"Agnir, you should know, my father—"

I hissed her quiet. I could not focus on a lecture.

Gunni thrust, and Onsgar parried. Onsgar's counter, and Gunni's cut. It was so simple to watch, even to me, even from this distance: testing blows to lure Onsgar into a mistake.

It was the wind. Jerking my braids, tugging my tunic, whipping a flurry of dust into the air. It caught Onsgar in the eye, and he winced, squinting against the debris. He didn't even see the thrust that took him.

Onsgar slid off Gunni's blade, clutching his middle.

"Brother!" I ran.

Onsgar stared up at me, doe-eyed, as I pressed together the wound in his middle. "Sister." His hands fumbled to press mine. My bracers were bloody on his wrists.

Above me, Gunni sputtered. "Is he— I didn't mean— I thought—"

Hadhnri knelt beside me and I shouldered her away. This was not for her. This was her fault.

"Onsgar." I kept my voice calm and reassuring. "You're all right. You're all right." Above him, I called frantically, "Father!"

Garadin Clan Fein was already at my side, cloth in his hands to stanch the blood, and he held his cheek against Onsgar's, kissing his brow.

"Well done, my child. Well done, Onsgar Second-Born Garadin Clan Fein."

A slight smile, dazed, cracked my brother's frightened face.

"Well done, brother," I echoed.

My father sobbed like a babe over the boy in his arms, and I buried my head into the crook of my father's shoulder.

Eventually, my father stood, lifting Onsgar in his arms. I saw then how the circle lingered, closed in on us. Pedhri Clan Aradoc stood behind Gunni, whose freckles stood starkly against his bloodless wet cheeks. Gunni's bloody sword hung heavy at his side. It dragged him down to his knees.

"I'm sorry," he whispered. To me, or to my father, I didn't know.

Without a word to Clan Aradoc, my father carried

my brother away and left me kneeling on the blood-slick grass.

I didn't realize that Hadhnri still knelt beside me until Pedhri Clan Aradoc frowned down at her. She shook her head, stubborn as ever, and he led Gunni away.

"Agnir?" Hadhnri said softly, when we were alone in the bloody grass. As alone as we could be amid the onlookers of the other clans. "Agnir, I am sorry. Forgive me. Forgive Gunni."

I said nothing.

"Please, Agnir. Look at me?" She tried to lean into my blurred vision, but I angled my head away. She would have had to crawl through Onsgar's death stain to meet my eyes.

She did not, and I said nothing.

"Agnir, please. There will be war. Can we not stop it, if we speak to our fathers?"

There would be no stopping this war. A child of Clan Aradoc had slain a child of Clan Fein. Our clans had fought for less. Right then, the burning in my heart called for vengeance, a wolf-howl of rage that dragged on and on within me, but I could not let it out. Not here, in front of Hadhnri. Only a choked whimper escaped.

Hadhnri glanced over her shoulder to where Pedhri beckoned sharply.

"Please, Agnir. Meet me at the spring at the full moon. If we can find it again, I know we can stop this."

She took my bloody hand in hers. "I wanted to tell you, my father—"

"Why didn't they protect him?" I whispered.

"I—I'm sorry. I only made them to protect *you*."

I pulled myself out of her grip, but she clung to me.

"Agnir, will you not hear me? He's going to send me away. To marry the Prince-Beyond-the-Fens."

I faced her, then, stunned by this new blow.

Tears stained Hadhnri's freckled cheeks, her eyes now hazel, now brown, glowing under sunlight and dimmed by the shadow of my body. The hard shell she had made for herself cracked open, leaving her turtle-soft. Here was the girl I'd made love to on Gunni's wedding night. Still there, and perhaps, still mine.

I stood as my father did, and left her kneeling in my brother's blood.

The Death-Oath

We bore Onsgar home to Fein land on a litter of wood and skins. Onsgar's mother, who was not my mother, keened beneath the burning sun when she saw him. Biudir's hairless chin trembled and he looked to me for an explanation. I turned from him and carried the litter with my father to the roundhouse while the pyre outside was prepared.

We washed him with fenswater and burned herbs until the roundhouse was smoky and bitter-scented. His mother knelt at his side while we worked, and her lamentations never ceased. The music of it gave rhythm to our own grief.

We burned him at sunset the next day, on a bed of peat, speaking stories of his young life, stories that I never knew because I was not there to witness them, because I was raised with the clan who killed him. They likened him to Bannos the Clever, and retold stories of Bannos with Onsgar in his stead. I had witnessed many death rites with Clan Aradoc, but I was never so intimately a part of them.

We feasted his honor, for he had died a warrior's death for the honor of Clan Fein, but I had not the stomach for it. We played music, with my father's voice loudest and carrying, a mournful baritone. Onsgar's mother's keening continued, a counterpoint to the drone of the bowharp. Her cry followed me every night into my dreams until I thought I would live with it always.

The pyre smoked through the next day, and the next, and on the third day, Garadin Clan Fein gathered us all together around the ashes of his child. He held a wooden bowl of fenswater.

"Pedhri Clan Aradoc." Garadin Clan Fein took a bellows-breath full of air to give him strength. He gripped the bowl tight in both hands. "He took two of my children from me. One has returned to us. The other will dwell ever more in the fens."

He turned to the ashes behind him and sprinkled some of the water over them with his hand, then scooped a handful into the bowl. He stirred it with two long fingers and held them up to all of us.

"I make this death-oath for Onsgar Second-Born Garadin Clan Fein. I will take from Pedhri Clan Aradoc what he has taken from me, or the luck-hound turn my own blade against me. He will lose a child, or I will wander the fens without bread, without water, without shelter, for the rest of my days."

He smeared a streak of Onsgar's muddied ashes across

his forehead, just as a clan member is marked for their oath to the clan.

"Who else will take this oath with me?"

I had never witnessed a death-oath before. I had supposed Garadin Clan Fein and Pedhri Clan Aradoc already held one against each other, given the strength of their hatred. I had also never thought that I would take a death-oath, but I felt the weight of Onsgar's body in my arms even now. The tackiness of his blood, like wet clay on my hands. Flakes of it still crusted my fingernails and the grooves of Hadhnri's bracers, though I'd cleaned them as best I could.

Biudir was already getting up from his knees, his chin jutting forward as he strode to our father on his gangly legs. He was three more Sunsteads away from becoming a full member of Clan Fein, but that didn't slow him.

I also wanted vengeance, and though I was confused, I felt shame as yet another brother showed more courage than me. I put a hand on his shoulder, holding him back so I could go to Garadin Clan Fein first. He followed close on my heel.

Garadin Clan Fein looked down on me gravely. Did he see inside my heart? I wondered. Did he see that this oath would break me? Did he understand that I loved both of Pedhri Clan Aradoc's children, and that this oath would bind me to end that? Was this yet another test?

I lowered my eyes as Garadin Clan Fein streaked my head with the mix of ashes and fenswater. The water was warm with the summer heat, the ashes gritty. The mixture tickled down the corner of my brow. I thought then how I wished I had kissed Hadhnri at the clan moot, at least once. (She was to marry the Prince-Beyond-the-Fens.) I thumbed the leather on my forearms, warm with that vague sense of her presence. I had thought she did not love me, but at the last, I saw the truth. Too late. And I could not go to the spring as she had asked—we had already looked for it once before and failed. I would not find it again.

None of this would have happened if Hadhnri had left the Making alone. Some of my anger was jealousy—she was brave enough to dare, even without me. To mark the world with her power. (She was to marry the Prince-Beyond-the-Fens.) It seemed like the only power I had was to bring death. Wherever I went, it followed. The clans were right. I was no symbol of greatness; I was born under the shade of ill-luck and lived under it still.

With the ash water on my forehead, I swore.

"By my name and my clan, Pedhri Clan Aradoc will lose a child to Clan Fein, and his debt to us be paid."

(She was to marry the Prince-Beyond-the-Fens.)

I walked from the pyre. Behind me, Biudir gave his oath earnestly, then my father-sisters. Even Onsgar's mother shrieked an oath to the sky.

Forgive me.

CLAN WAR

The Baneswood

Preparations for war went quickly. So quickly that it became clear to me that they had been underway for much longer than I realized. Visitors from Clans Pall and Hanarin came ever more frequently from the other side of the Baneswood, barricading themselves with my father in the roundhouse. They spoke of supplies and alliances. They spoke of fear and defeat.

The bowyer braved the Baneswood to gather deadfall from its yews, and the geese were plucked for fletching.

Solwin's anvil rang day and night and the grindstone rasped its harmony.

I began making armor.

All the while, I watched the moon wax in her sky. She seemed closer to us every day, pus-swollen with a sickly yellow turn to her light. The tales go that she and the sun were once lovers until a bitter feud divided them into day and night. Only when she was weak and waning could the sun stomach sharing the same sky. The tales made me think on Hadhnri—as if I'd been able to stop since I last saw her on the killing field. I hated her for what her

Making had driven us to. I wished I had touched her in tenderness.

(She was to marry the Prince-Beyond-the-Fens.)

When I wasn't caught by the moon, or my impossible longing, the Baneswood called to me. No longer as delicate as spider silk, its insistent tug guided me by the chin. Sucked at my heels. More than once, I tripped and startled from a daze only to find myself halfway out of the hamlet. Halfway to heeding that call.

To save myself, I worked.

The work, however, no longer soothed me. Some days, I worked my craft in desperation, certain that my leatherwork would be the difference between a clan member's life and their death: protection from the pierce of an arrow, the surety of a blade at the hip.

Other days, I worked in bitterness. I did not choose this war for myself, and yet it had caught me in its grip, torn between the things I most wanted in the world. I remembered the way everyone looked at me at the moot. I was branded by their gaze. In becoming Garadin Clan Fein's symbol, I lost my own will.

And yet, symbol as I was, I was powerless.

At that thought, my hands froze on the leather on the table. I heard her voice: *Think of what we could do.*

Needle to leather, I tried to lose myself in the meditative action.

What if it's a gift?

I yelped and brought my bleeding thumb to my

mouth and sucked it clean. I watched it well up again, gleaming and red, a bright, fat bead. The cord tying me to the Baneswood thickened, grew tighter between one throbbing heartbeat and the next. A rising tide within me— *No.*

It was a dark gift. I did not want it.

The tide went out, leaving me with a disappointment not unlike an aborted climax. I shuddered and wiped the blood away on my trousers and finished sewing the beaten metal round onto the jerkin.

I told myself, I would never find the spring.

I told myself, I would not betray my clan. My blood clan. My true clan, true as it was tattooed upon my cheek.

I told myself, I would face her on the battlefield and not before.

I told myself, I did not care where she was or who she wed.

I told myself lie upon lie upon lie until the moon was near bursting, when I snuck out of Clan Fein's roundhouse with my bracers on and the screaming dagger at my hip.

The Baneswood separated the small parcel of dry land that belonged to Clan Fein from the bigger island of Clan Aradoc. East of the wood and north some were Clans Pall and Hanarin, each only a bit bigger than Clan Fein. North and west a bit, Clan Elyin, and they were alone on the other side of Aradoc, so it made sense that they would hide behind the Aradoc shield rather than fight them alone. My father had sent someone to sway them; it would have been good to grip Aradoc between two fingers and squeeze. The messenger never returned.

I hovered at the edge of the trees, the pale birch bark glowing in the night, the fog swirling at my bare shins. The shadows between the trees were impenetrable. The call was a shriek in my soul and to stand there unmoving took all my strength. My jaw ached with the clenching of it.

How had I ever been brave enough to step into the fates-bane's wood?

Oh, but that answer came easily. Brave Hadhnri. I would follow her anywhere.

With one step, I surrendered to that rising tide.

The wood was dark and silent at times. At others, the sound of night insects and rustling leaves deafened me until I spun myself around, trying to see through the thickness of the foliage. My only compass was the binding around my heart that pulled me ever deeper.

"Hadhnri?" I called more than once, and more than once I was met with the flurry of something underbrush or overhead. Only once I heard a distorted cry that I thought was my name. I followed that sound and almost fell into a dark chasm.

Backing away from the edge, I caught my breath from panic. I gripped my hands around my forearms, holding my bracers as if they were a talisman. Would they protect me against the fates-bane itself?

Or, came the worse thought, *what if the Baneswood has already taken Hadhnri?*

"Hadhnri?" I whispered, this time a prayer. I had no idea how long I had been walking; the trees knit themselves tight overhead to shield the round-bellied moon from view. So I repeated her name under my breath, clutching the bracers and thinking of that sun-speckled spring and our first cold-water kiss. I followed the leash of the luck-hound.

"Agnir."

I heard my name again, faint, and turned hesitantly. I stepped toward the voice, warier for my earlier missteps.

"Hadhnri?"

"Agnir?" It came again, and I swore it was her voice, rippling with the undercurrent of water. My fear of the fates-bane was too strong for me to rush toward it, even though the pull was almost unbearable.

"Hadhnri?"

"Agnir!" Hadhnri crashed from the trees to my right and stopped, bracing herself on her knees as she heaved breath. She squinted at me skeptically from her hunched position. "Agnir? Is that you?"

I stepped toward her, hand raised. "Hadhnri? You're alive! Are you all right?"

She straightened and reached for the seax at her hip. "Agnir? Truly?"

I halted and held the hilt of my own dagger. "Hadhnri, it's me."

What had she seen in the darkness to make her doubt? Or was it always her plan to ambush me in the cursed dark?

"How did I get the scar on my lip?" she asked, advancing one careful step.

"I gave it to you," I said, smug in the memory despite my wariness. "You have a slow guard from the left. Or at least, you did."

"Agnir." Hadhnri dropped her hand to her side and closed the space between us.

I didn't know whether to run into her arms or keep her at a distance. I had forgotten neither the scalding of her anger nor my own.

Instead of choosing, I cocked my head. "Is that the spring?"

The gurgle of water was an easier thing to seize upon than the whip-tail of my feelings. With ginger, sidelong steps, I led the way down the tumble of forest litter to where the sound was loudest.

The small clearing let in the moon's sick-yellow light, and I could see a pool of water, its slow trickle. The spring was different now, and I struggled to recall how it looked when we were children. I could only remember how it felt: the pleasant coolness in the hot weather, on our sweaty skin. The sweetness of the clean water, more pure than anything I'd drunk before or since.

The call of the fates-bane was silent.

"It looks different," Hadhnri said, stopping beside me.

FATE'S BANE

Her body was warm in the summer night. Sunstead was a month gone, and Ha'night seemed an age away. Still, the night was brisk and the pool frigid. Instead of refreshing, it put me in mind of the cold of a corpse.

"We shouldn't be here." I stepped back but bumped into her.

She steadied me even as I tried to pull away. Before I could march back the way I came, she tightened her hand on my arm and said, "Please, Agnir. Will you not stay a moment with me?"

In the moonlight, her face was carved in anguish.

"Please. I don't want to go to war with you."

The war had gone from my mind. It seemed a silly thing, in the clutches of the fates-bane, but now the anger of the past month boiled in me, even damped by the darkness.

"My brother would still be alive if you had kept your word to me, Hadhnri Clan Aradoc."

"And my own brother would be dead, or my father." Hadhnri glared down at me. I felt the surge of her rage in the rise and fall of her chest. "Or do you still claim that no one in Clan Fein snuck to our bedrolls in the night? A tryst gone wrong, was it?"

"Will *you* pretend your father isn't planning to give our lands away to some woman who has never even seen them?" I growled into her face. "For what? What will he gain? Clan Fein, exterminated? Cleared out like vermin by her heralds and their soldiers?"

Hadhnri closed her eyes. She had not released my arm. We were so close that I could feel the cool breath of her resignation.

"I am sorry your brother is dead, Agnir," Hadhnri said, her voice thick, "but I cannot—" She shook her head. "I cannot lie to you and say I wish it were otherwise. I— Gunni—Gunni has a daughter now—"

"Stop. Please, stop." Salt laced my lips. How could I hate her when her truth was my own? I sagged into her chest and she caught me, held me in her strength while I wept.

"Agnir, sweet Agnir," she whispered in my ear, over and over. "Sweet Agnir, my love."

"Do not marry the prince," I sobbed against her chest.

"Sit with me. Talk with me."

Hadhnri slid her hand down my arm to my own hand, and when I didn't pull away, she led me to the stones beside the spring. There was the cold I remembered. I shivered in my sleeveless tunic. Only then did I notice that Hadhnri carried a pack, and from it, she pulled a blanket and draped it over my shoulders. She held the ends of it on either side of my shoulders and searched my face. Her eyes found my lips.

I turned away, as if I hadn't craved that kiss these last long years.

"How do we stop this war?" I huddled deeper into the wool.

"We could ask our fathers to marry us off to each other. Unite the clans, at last."

I snorted with disdain and Hadhnri flinched.

"You didn't think it was so cursed an idea before," she muttered.

"My entire clan has sworn a death-oath to take from your father what he took from mine." The muddy ash had dried on our foreheads, where we left it until it fell away. "*I* swore a death-oath, may the—may the luckhound turn my blade against me." A shudder crossed my spine to even mention the fates-bane here, at the seat of its power.

Hadhnri gaped at me, stricken. "But Gunni is your brother too. And I'm—" She broke off abruptly.

"Is he my brother?" I spat into her hurt silence. "He kept us apart as much as Pedhri Clan Aradoc. He never saw me worthy of you." This old bitter kernel had grown roots since Sunstead. "I'm not a child anymore, Hadhnri. I can see things for what they were." I sifted my hand through the detritus, chasing the break-joint crack of twigs. "What they are."

"Am I childish then, Agnir Clan Fein, to have hope still?" Hadhnri said softly. "To remember the oath we made?" She turned to me, moonlight catching on her damp cheeks.

The love in her eyes dried the angry retort on my tongue. It was honest and broken, held together with sheer will—how could I pretend I did not match it? If only I could capture her love and hold it to my chest forever. With gentle thumbs, I brushed away her tears and brought her face to mine. She held me fast as I kissed her softly. We pulled apart to ask the silent question.

The answer was music, a music I knew down to the marrow of me. The moan of the bull deer. The bark of the fox. How to mend what was broken? The drumming of the clans against Hadhnri's ribs. The pipes in my ear. We were a Made thing, as much as any leather wrought. Steady fingers, the rise and fall of the needle. Blood in the mouth. War was coming, but I was not alone anymore. They could not take the fens from us—not the dragonflies, not the Baneswood; not the rush of the Ene or its floods. *Hadhnri, will you forgive me?* We were a Making. That warmth in my stomach. Wet flesh under the thumb. The rightness of a stitch placed true. The needle piercing through. Tightening around the throat. Here where we began, we could unmake it all: What if we told them how the luck-hound dogged us? Would the truth mend what was broken? *Will you still fly crow-sure to a cold-stone prince with nothing to offer but soft metal?* Our warmth rising in my stomach. Would the war still come? Its hot breath on our necks, sharp steel in our backs. I had always been alone. *Will you go, Hadhnri?* A curse. Blinding warmth. The needle piercing through.

The Choice

"Take me," Hadhnri said quietly into my braids.

"Again?" I startled from the languid haze of our after. "You're not finished?"

She stroked a thumb along my bare neck. No collar stopped her kissing me there, long and lingering. The spring bubbled at our heads.

"Steal me from my father. We'll run away."

I considered it only a moment longer than I had the last time she asked me, so long ago.

"Your father would still blame me, and my father yours. Unless he knows I went willing, and he will not believe it unless he sees it."

"Then I'll go back with you, tonight."

I let myself entertain that too: escorting Hadhnri back to Clan Fein, telling my father we were wedded—that we had been for years, though there'd been no one to witness our oath but the trees and the fens and the fates-bane itself. No matter how I twisted the vision in my mind, I could see nothing but the hatred in his eyes and the smudge across his forehead. He would not have

Hadhnri in his clan, no matter how it wounded Pedhri Clan Aradoc or ruined his plans for the Fens.

"I have been thinking. I came because—" With great effort, I let the words rush out. "We should use it. The Makings. You were right. If this is the only way I can touch the world, then—then I will. I'll grab it by the throat if I must. I want to be my own, for once."

Hadhnri stared at me, resting on one elbow, mouth open in surprise. My cheeks warmed, embarrassed by my fervor. I waited for her to speak, to say anything at all. Instead, she stroked the bracers at my forearms and looked to the dagger on the belt I had discarded.

I dug into the cool, soft earth with my fingers. The moon above was no longer sick-yellow but bright as the silver torc round Hadhnri's neck. The chirp and buzz and rustle of the insects and animals who dwelt here had gone faint, as if their domain stopped at the edge of the clearing, which was ours and ours alone. Only I did not think it was.

I pushed myself up, slithered to the edge of the spring, and plunged my hand inside. It was colder than I remembered. I closed my eyes and let it run between my fingers.

"Are we cursed?" I asked through clenched teeth, trying not to shiver.

Hadhnri joined me in the water, twining her hand in mine. I shivered anyway.

"It doesn't feel like a curse." She squeezed my hand

beneath the water and I opened my eyes to see her staring at me.

The luck-hound wasn't known for giving gifts. Not in any of the tales I'd heard told. And yet ... everything we'd ever Made together had an element of ill-luck. And I couldn't deny that she had some point—nothing ill had happened to *us*. I pulled our hands out of the water and kissed her chill knuckles. I licked the water from my lips. It tasted of apples. It tasted of Hadhnri, the salt of her sweat, her pleasure.

"What if *we* are a Making?" I murmured.

I did not realize I'd spoken aloud until Hadhnri hummed a question.

"What if it was the spring that brought us together," I continued, "you for me, and me for you?"

Hadhnri brought my own knuckles to her lips, her tongue flicking against them, teasing, tickling like a fish. There were no fish in the spring. She smirked, and I wondered what she tasted. But her voice was serious when she turned my face up to hers.

"I've made one true choice in my life, Agnir—do not take it away from me." She kissed me slowly. "I loved you the moment I saw you in the dark, with the slaves—before I even knew what love was. And when I learned, I loved you all the more."

Far from reassuring me, her words rang even more sharply of fate. She described something out of our hands, moving us without our knowing better. Without the fates-bane's own luck, her father would not have raided mine when he did, and I would not have been taken ward. I would not have known her as anything more than Hadhnri Second-Born Pedhri Clan Aradoc, child of my father's enemy. Not simply as Hadhnri, *my* Hadhnri.

I said none of that. I would not take that choice from her, because I wanted it just as badly.

"Then what will we do?" I asked, turning the subject back. "We build a workshop in the Baneswood?"

"We can Make what we need on our own. If you remember me. I—I think of you, when I work. Sometimes it is enough."

She sat up and reached for my dagger before reconsidering. She took up her own instead and cut off a new lock of hair, wrapped it around her finger, and then pushed it into my hand. Then she ran her fingers through my braids.

"May I?" she asked.

I nodded, and she cut the end of one. "And then?"

"And then . . ." Hadhnri hesitated, as if only now realizing how we tempted fate. "We arm our clans with the luck-hound's gifts."

The Warning

We parted, eventually, after loving each other again and drinking from the spring in great, thirsty gulps. The journey home was oddly easy—or perhaps I was too drunk with the feel of Hadhnri on my skin to notice the tangles the trail led me down until it spat me out on familiar ground. I picked my way through the wetland at the borders of Clan Fein, feeling Hadhnri's absence, and at the same time, full of her warmth.

What did the fates-bane know of love, I wondered? We told no tales of that.

I froze in the dark at the sound of a buzzard call. A warning. I responded with the hoot of a marsh owl, and the sentries on guard made themselves visible.

"Agnir?" said one. It was Solwin. How beautiful she was, with arms thicker than Hadhnri's and a chin as hard as her anvil. And yet.

"Solwin," I hailed her and continued toward home.

"Where have you been?" she asked, cutting a zagged path to intercept me. The coolness of her voice surprised me.

I gave the lie I'd planned: "I wanted to walk in the woods. It calms me. I didn't go far, don't worry."

Her scowl deepened. How well did she remember the night she had to finish my watch, or that ill-luck journey home from Clan Hanarin?

"You were gone a thre'night," Solwin growled.

My mouth dropped open, all pretense gone. I jerked around to find the moon, and yes, fine slivers had been shaved off her coin. I stared dumbly at Solwin and she took my arm roughly.

"I'm to take you to Garadin Chief."

Solwin marched me to the roundhouse, where the fires were still burning. Garadin Clan Fein stood from his great chair when Solwin brought me in.

"Agnir?" He came hesitantly toward me, flanked by all three of my father-sisters.

"Father." I freed my arm from Solwin's and knelt before my father.

"My own dear one." He knelt to meet me and whispered, "Where were you, Agnir First-Born Garadin Clan Fein?"

The keen, dangerous edge of his voice slid against my ear.

"I was in the Baneswood, Father," I said. Those in the roundhouse gasped.

Garadin Fein looked around us, nostrils flaring. He got up and left the roundhouse, and I followed back into the night. Insects buzzed above the water and frogs plopped in and out. We heard the tinny squeaks of bats and even the odd bark of a fox. And of course, the noise of the clan's evening: the food, the laughter, the grumbling complaints, the last of the chores.

When we were alone—almost alone; I heard Laudir-father-sister's deliberate footsteps behind me—he said, "We sent a search party into the Baneswood. They didn't find you."

I thought of the way the paths twisted and turned. If the fates-bane did not wish me found, no one would have found me.

"It's where I was, Father."

"For a thre'night?" Laudir said, her voice as hard as Solwin's. Her trust had been the hardest of my father-sisters to earn. I thought I had won it with the gift of the wide belt she wore at her waist, but apparently that was not so. "What were you doing there? What did you eat?"

"I was looking for the fates-bane, as Bannos the Clever once did." The lie came to my tongue after only a moment. "I thought I would see if the tales were true. If I could win it to our side in the fight to come."

Laudir's eyes narrowed. She looked to my father for his response. He studied me with dark eyes that mirrored my own, then he jerked his head at Laudir. Back toward the roundhouse. She frowned between the two of us but obeyed.

"You met that dog's whelp at the moot. You spoke to her."

I glanced to his side, expecting to see Onsgar, hangdog guilty. But Onsgar was gone to ash and spilled into the fens.

"What did you tell her of our plans, girl?"

"Nothing, Father, on my name and my clan, nothing!" I flinched, expecting the break-jaw crack of knuckles against my cheek that I'd not felt for years. Something in my father's face changed. I couldn't say *softened*, for his sharp jaw still clenched and his face still twisted in a half snarl, but change it did.

"Did you find it? The fates-bane."

"I . . . didn't think I did. But I didn't know I'd been gone for so long. Maybe it found me."

"Are you well?" He looked me up and down, especially my eyes.

I almost told him, then. I almost asked him if he would consider the death-oath paid if our fasting brought Hadhnri into Clan Fein. But the knife-edge glint in his eye reminded me too much of Aradoc-Father's, right before the blow. I could imagine him asking me, *Who would fast themselves to an enemy of Clan Fein?*

No, the old, bitter lesson remained. Better, always, to keep my heart hidden.

I stared back, both eyes wide open. "I have them both," I said, though I covered the eye without my clan mark.

My father smiled, like a bird's shadow flying over the moon.

The Battle

For the next month, I endured Laudir-father-sister's sidelong scowls. She would not trust me again. But I took her plain leather jerkin and pressed in a new design. It was not as cleanly beautiful as it would have been if Hadhnri had done the cutting, but I clutched that twist of her hair in one fist as I worked and would have sworn to the luck-hound itself that I could feel her beside me, feel the warm glow of our Making.

"For luck," I told Laudir, when I handed it back with a bow. "For Clan Fein."

She eyed me with suspicion but ran her thumb along the work appreciatively. I say it was not so good as Hadhnri's, but my skill was no little thing.

Laudir's jerkin was not the only thing I worked in that month of preparation. I sank my wishes into resoled boots, carved them into the hafts of hammers and axes, pressed them into scabbards and belts, and sewed them into shirts and trousers and one unlucky pair of undergarments that hung on the line within my reach.

Wishes or curses or prayers, I still couldn't say what they were, or whose work I did. I didn't know how they would manifest. I thought too often of the herald's man, imagining his purple, unbreathing face. I could only hope and whisper as I worked, *This is not to harm. Give us peace. This is not to harm.* I played the luck-hound's game, and who knew how our luck would turn? I knew only that my dread grew and grew, and I couldn't tell if it was for the coming battle or something of the fates-bane itself, stealing over me as I took of its power.

When I faltered, I thumbed the dry lock of Hadhnri's hair and thought of her working too.

We marched the moon before second Ha'night, circling the Baneswood to the west and linking with Clans Hanarin and Pall. Fog rose, swirling about our boots, following us. The air was humid, but when the sun rose properly, it would burn the fog away. From there, we turned to the great island in the fens where Clan Aradoc had its sheep and its farms, its people who never hungered. Nothing gnawed my belly today but fear.

Clans Aradoc and Elyin waited atop the hill, and in the sunless gray dawn, I made out Pedhri Clan Aradoc with Hadhnri, a shorter figure with no-less-brilliant red hair. Gunni was beside him, too, and a host of other figures whose shapes I could easily guess at. Of course I could; they had been my clan, once.

I stood behind a line of shieldsmen, beside my father and my father-sisters. Biudir shifted anxiously at my side. I didn't have to be there; my father said I could stay with the other craftsmen back in the village. But he was wrong. Hadhnri was here, and so I would be. The leather bracers were warm on my arms. When I left her in the Baneswood, she made me promise to wear them, no matter what. I didn't know what to believe, only that she and I had trusted our fate and the fate of our clans to all our Makings. At the very least, I could have faith in Hadhnri's bracers. In Hadhnri's love.

As long as Hadhnri lives.

"When does it start?" Biudir whispered.

"I don't know," I said.

Laudir-father-sister shushed us.

Across the way, Hadhnri gestured toward us in a goose-feather frenzy, then at her father. I could not see her face, only the shape, but they were not a family given to subtle gestures. Tall and broad as my love was, she was still smaller than her father, but she balked not, even when he cut her words in half with a firm slice of his hand.

"Ready yourselves." Garadin Clan Fein held an arm cocked in the air, two fingers up. The shield line before us braced.

As Pedhri Clan Aradoc raised his horn to his lips, Hadhnri leapt between him and us, dragging his arm down. Pedhri shook his daughter off, but she pushed him back, shouting. Whatever she said made him pause and stare at our line, the horn in his hand forgotten.

Hadhnri went to her knees, and I knew every word of her confession, though I couldn't hear it.

Oh Hadhnri, brave Hadhnri.

Pedhri raised his horn again, and this time, Gunni held Hadhnri back, offering her his own rough words as she struggled.

Pedhri Clan Aradoc blew his war horn and no sound came out. He looked down at it, baffled, as every dog in the village began to bark and howl. Again, he blew; the dogs increased their madness. The Aradoc archers lowered their bows in confusion and looked to their leader. Hadhnri looked toward me, and I knew it for a second confession.

Or, I thought I did. It might have been the warning for what she did next.

Oh Hadhnri, foolish Hadhnri.

She broke free of Gunni's grasp and sprinted straight for me.

"Now!" cried Garadin Clan Fein. "For Clan Fein! For the true heirs of Bannos!"

He charged, and with him my father-sisters and my youngest brother. With my stone-fruit throat, I followed, praying to reach Hadhnri first.

Pedhri threw the horn to the ground and cried to his archers, but his voice barely carried. In uncoordinated waves, they pulled and they aimed and they loosed. The shieldsmen ahead of us braced and we clammed up tight behind their wall.

An arrow flew true for Laudir-father-sister's breast, and I cried out as I watched it hit the jerkin I'd tooled. Her face contorted with pain and that regret that comes with knowing you've died sooner than you wanted. But the arrow did not sink into her chest. It caromed into the arm of my father beside her. He grunted and yanked the arrow from its shallow hold in the swell of his muscle. He moved his axe to his other hand and glanced, bewildered, at Laudir. Laudir, however, looked behind my father to me.

"For luck," I mouthed. She frowned and rubbed her chest.

By then, instead of burning away with the morning, the fog swirled densely at our hips, rising quickly. We ran again. Arrows again. Shields again. And then we were too close for arrows, and the clans mingled in a way only battle and clan moots would allow.

I had to get to Hadhnri.

I shouted for her as I had in the Baneswood, but my voice was drowned by the crash of fighting around me. I was loath to hurt anyone—I'd lived with our enemy almost my whole life. They'd taught me everything I knew, the good and the ill.

The same feeling did not stay their blades.

I ducked around an axe that came swinging out of the fog that obscured everything but the person in front of me. I recognized him. Gurdhri, who had sung the songs of Bannos to me and Hadhnri and the other Aradoc children while he turned meat over the fire. Gurdhri, who had never tweaked my ear because I never stole meat from the spit like the other children, who would cut me off a small piece and shoo me away with a smile.

"Gurdhri, please!" I held my hands up, my seax dangling slack.

Gurdhri's eyebrows rose. He looked older now, but the years had been kind. They'd given him a soft belly and deep lines of laughter. The laugh-lines turned as he recognized me too.

"I'll make it quick, girl. A knock on the head and you'll sleep until it's over. I'm sorry." And certain, he looked it.

He reached for me and I jumped back, but the ground beneath my feet was marsh-soft where it should have been solid. I knew the Aradoc land as well as any, but not today. Not with the fates-bane at its work. On faun-legs, I fell.

I found my nose at his boots. Boots I recognized. Boots with a raven-knot I had drawn and watched Hadhnri chase with her awl. They spun a tight little round as Gurdhri searched for me, but I was blanketed by the fog.

"Gurdhri!"

Gurdhri stopped and I grasped his boot. Gurdhri, who was too shy to dance with Theitri no matter how she winked at him, until Hadhnri and I had made him boots to wing his feet.

I held his boot and felt the warmth of the Making we had done, and *called* to it.

The boot jerked out of my hand, almost kicking me in the face. I rolled to my own feet and saw his fear-wide eyes as his legs spasmed against his will.

"By the left eye, what have you done to me, girl?"

"Please, Gurdhri. I need to find Hadhnri." Only together could we beg our fathers to stop this.

Who would fast themselves to an enemy of Clan Fein?
I would, Father. I would.

I left Gurdhri dancing in the fog behind me and shouted for Hadhnri again.

The fog was so thick now that I knew it for the fatesbane's doing. The full weight of its ill-balanced hand lay upon us. All around me, fighters struggled against our Makings. A man with Clan Elyin's split-moon beneath his eye sat on the ground, his face long with despair, his axes forgotten at his side. A woman of Clan Pall knelt in the mud, clutching her hand to her ears and begging someone to be quiet, please, *please*. Another woman swatted at the bite-flies that swarmed to her leather helm.

Our Makings were working, but our plan had not succeeded. Not yet.

"Hadhnri!" I called again, willing the fog to part for me, as Gurdhri's shoes had danced at my command, but I had not Made the fog, and it was not mine to command.

"Agnir!"

Gunni First-Born Pedhri Clan Aradoc emerged from

the fog before me. Blood speckled his face and smeared his hands. His face was twisted in a rabid-dog sneer.

My knees went soft.

He swung at me and I fell to the side, narrowly missing a blow meant to cleave me from shoulder to hip.

Gunni has a daughter now.

"Brother! Please." *Please, please, please.* How often I had said that word today, and how often it had been ignored. "You once called me sister. Will you listen to me? Where is Hadhnri?"

The fury in Gunni's face faltered, and his sword slammed to the ground. Hope skipped in my chest. The hilt grip I had Made still wrapped his age-day gift. He snarled in frustration and yanked the sword up to point at me again, but I could see the effort it took to hold it in the strain of his forearms. The luck-hound was with me.

"'Sister?' You betrayed us. We fight today because of *you*."

"You killed Onsgar at the clan moot," I growled. "You knew what this would do to the clans!" I felt the crack of the dried ashes on my forehead as if it were only yesterday I had made my death-oath against Pedhri Clan Aradoc. Against Gunni Clan Aradoc.

A glimpse of anguish turned Gunni into the boy I'd seen at the dueling ground. His sword slammed back to the ground. He yanked in vain to raise it. "I asked him to yield," he whispered.

"He was my brother. He was an heir of Clan Fein. Please, Gunni, tell me where she is."

He shook his head. "You do not deserve her, Agnir Clan Fein. She is too brave, too loyal for a Fein snake like you. She will do her duty to our clan and unite us in peace with the Queen-Beyond-the-Fens." His muscles bunched as he ripped his sword up again. It seemed lighter this time, and he brought it high.

His words cut. They would not have, if some part of me did not agree. I spoke anyway, through my sudden tears.

"Against her will? Though she is already wed to me?"

He hesitated, straining beneath the blade's desire to plummet. "You should have known your place, Agnir."

As Gunni's blade swung down toward my head, I reached for the luck-hound's cord, the cord binding me to Hadhnri.

I shut my eyes. I whispered her name.

The End

Poor girl. Oh, you silly child. Run you then to your true love's side. She calls for you.

It is the fate of lovers. To call. To come.

But what can you do when fate's terrible blade swings toward her throat?

How quickly can love carry you?

And when you are too late?

When you learn that even heroes cannot forsake their fates?

You will drown your grief in the River Ene, where we all began and where everything, even stories, even magic, even love, at last must end.

Or Maybe, the Tale Goes like This

Once, a girl fell in love with her father's ward, and they plighted their troth in the luck-hound's wood.

But their clans went to war, as all and fate knew they should, and the girl who had been ward was now a woman grown, marked with the ink of her true-blood clan.

Bold as Bannos, Agnir Clan Fein stood against her foster brother as he made to hew her down, but strength of arms was not her strength. If battle was not her blessing, it was the fates-bane's own luck that she had mastered. Her brother who was not her brother held a sword she'd bound with guilt, and on her arms she bore a promise: She could not be harmed, so long as her true love yet lived.

And Hadhnri Clan Aradoc did live; she sprinted 'cross the sucking fens, without heed for the luck-hound's treacherous gaps. She cried out only once, clear as the anvil-strike:

"Agnir!"

Clever as Bannos, Hadhnri Clan Aradoc threw her

own blade at her brother's feet, where it stuck, point down, in the mud. He turned his eye upon her, and where he looked, his blade followed.

They say she ran upon that bloody point by accident, but if so—why did she smile with her last breath?

They say Agnir Clan Fein's anguish echoed through the land, and even the Queen-Beyond-the-Fens in her cold-stone halls on her cold-metal chair wept, though she did not know the reason.

They say that Gunni Clan Aradoc, that slayer of kin, knelt in Hadhnri Clan Aradoc's blood as Garadin Clan Fein ran upon him with death-oath sworn and no mercy in his heart.

They say Agnir rose silently from the fens like the luck-hound itself and stood alone between them, her open hands full of grief.

As long as I live, swore her love in the Baneswood—but Hadhnri's blood was nothing now but lacquer upon leather.

And her father did not stop, and her brother did not rise, and Agnir Clan Fein did not move.

So she fell, curled like a shield over her lover, where she died in the fens of Bannos.

Or Perhaps,
the Tale Goes like This

Once, a girl fell in love with her father's ward, and they plighted their troth in the luck-hound's wood.

With their bond came a gift—which may not have been a gift but a curse—which may not have been a curse, only luck—which may not have been any of these things at all—that held the destiny of all on that field. They snared even themselves in the web of their Makings, caught between the young warrior with the heavy soul and that chief burning bright with vengeance.

Their love spelled the doom of Clan Aradoc.

Their love meant the end of Clan Fein.

And how did they end, these great clans of Bannos, these rulers of all the fens?

They say Gunni Clan Aradoc's blade drove itself into the earth when his sisters two knelt at his feet, held tight in the fates-bane's grip. They say when Garadin Clan Fein brought his sword up to settle his death oath, his own daughter Agnir rose from her knees to the sound of a hundred hundred starlings, and their music gave wing to her voice:

"Father, please. I love them. Will you spare their lives for me?"

"His child's life to answer mine," said he. "So we swore it by the fates-bane."

Agnir the Bold did not waver between her father's blade and her brother's, with her wife's strong heart beating against her back.

"I cannot kill one brother to answer the death of the other. I will not," said she. "Discharge the oath and claim my wife kin. Take his child as your own." As she had dreamed in the Baneswood with Hadhnri, so could it be. Hadhnri took her hand.

"You are a snake who bites both ways," said Laudir Clan Fein, who did not trust. She turned her blade on Hadhnri, and Agnir stepped between, her father-sister's seax against her breast.

The chieftain's voice cut between them. "You would fast yourself to an enemy of Clan Fein?"

"I would, Father. I have. Under the eye of the luck-hound itself."

They say that the sight of the lovers' clasped hands softened the heart of that grieving father. They say he was weeping when Pedhri Clan Aradoc's arrow pierced his right eye, and that Agnir flew to him as he fell.

But they also say that Laudir Clan Fein did not weep for love of her brother-daughter, nor did she weep for her brother and his shrike-spear agonies. They say her rage jagged like a heron's beak, once, twice, thrice, and that

Gunni Clan Aradoc dug his own barrow as he failed to raise his blade.

And they say Hadhnri Clan Aradoc wept blood over his body in those brackish fields of Bannos until Pedhri Clan Aradoc came, not with knuckles but with axes bared to kill the kin of Garadin Fein—that girl who had once been his ward.

And that Hadhnri raised her brother's sword—lighter in her hands than a willow leaf—to her own father's throat, saying, "Let it be done, Father. Let it end."

And that chief of all chiefs laid his cold weapons down in the bloody red fens of Bannos.

The Tale We Tell

They called it the trickster, they called it the luck-hound, they called it the fates-bane, but none now can say what is true.

Was it Hadhnri Clan Aradoc who fell, her own brother who delivered the blow? Or did Garadin Fein perish when his own daughter held back his hate?

Was it Agnir the Clever and Hadhnri the Bold who turned the clans' fates with their Makings? Or did fate make a Making of them?

Why did the fates-bane reach out its hand to tangle the threads of its conqueror's heirs?

Are these the questions that matter as you wend your way through these woods?

In the seat of Bannos's power, over the bloodied bodies and the sharpened steel, where the earth is richest and the peat plentiful, two women swore an oath by the fates-bane and united the clans with their love.

This is the tale as we heard it from our fathers and our father-sisters.

FATE'S BANE

This is the tale as we heard it from our mothers and our mother-brothers.

This is the tale, say the lore-makers and the tale-tellers of Clan Bannos.

This is the tale, say the song-singers of Clan Bannos.

This is the tale of the Fens.

ACKNOWLEDGMENTS

Fate's Bane's short length doesn't diminish the work that went into it. To that end, I would like to thank the professionals: my agent, Mary C. Moore, for having faith in every ending I write, happy or tragic; my editor, Carl Engle-Laird, for challenging me and keeping me honest with the work, and Matt Rusin; to the production, marketing, and publicity teams—you have my deepest gratitude for championing this book.

This book would also be nothing without the synergy of other artists, so first let me thank my cover artist, Mary Metzger, for making my sad swamp lesbians so tragically beautiful, and to Christine Foltzer for the design; I could stare at them all day, and in fact, I have more than once. This book has also been full of music from its inception, so thank you to Loreena McKennitt, whose music has always made me want to tell stories, and Gealdýr, whose album *Vígríðr* became the unofficial soundtrack for this novella in my head.

To get properly in spirit for the work, I also needed to get my hands dirty: thank you to the crew at Woodland

Acknowledgments

Ways for teaching me the ropes of bushcraft, especially my instructors Rich, Dan, Rob, Michaela, Mike, Paul, and Kat.

Thank you to all of the authors who generously read early and provided blurbs. Especially especially Alix E. Harrow for swapping manuscripts with me and supporting the ambitious triple-threat endings. Go read *The Everlasting*! Thanks also to the writers who wrote with me, commiserated with me, in coffee shops and online, especially Grace Curtis, Ben Schroder, Tasha Suri, Lee Mandelo, Shelley Parker-Chan, Kate Dylan, Hannah Kaner, Saara El-Arifi, Samantha Shannon, K. A. Doore, Melissa Caruso, Devin Madson, and Jess Barber. Your irreverence is more valuable than you know.

Finally, thank you to S, who did all of the above and more. (Except for the music. And the bushcraft.)

ABOUT THE AUTHOR

C. L. Clark is a British Fantasy Award–winning editor and the Nebula Award–nominated author of a handful of books, several short stories, and a few essays, including the Magic of the Lost trilogy (beginning with *The Unbroken*) and the *Arcane* novel *Ambessa: Chosen of the Wolf*. When she's not imagining the fall of empires, she's trying not to throw her kettlebells through the walls.